MODEL SPY

THE SPECIALISTS BOOK ONE

SHANNON GREENLAND

NOWHERE TO RUN. NOWHERE TO HIDE

The entire greenhouse brightened with white light, and a shrill siren went off.

David grabbed my hand, and we took off down the path.

A mile later, we burst through the trees on the outskirts of an Ushbanian town, a different one from where the modeling school and hotel were located.

A police siren pierced the air. David grabbed my hand and yanked me down an alley. We ran past a Dumpster and skidded to a halt when a police car pulled in the opposite end. David backed me up against the side of a building and plastered his body to mine. Our chests heaved against each other with winded breaths.

He buried his mouth against my ear. "Wrap. Your. Arms. Around. Me."

I did as he instructed, my heart hammering, keeping the police car in my peripheral vision. It slowly rolled toward us. "It's coming," I hissed, desperately trying to think of what to do next.

"Sorry," he mumbled right before crushing his mouth to mine.

Oh my God, I'm sixteen, and I've never been kissed. Please let me be doing this right.

ONE

<!ENTITY % phrase "em"[ ]>
   <!Element (%styfon;~%phse;)- -(%line:)>
   <(&#xOOOC;)-(&#x0009)-(𠀋)>
   "No, no, no," I muttered to myself.
   <!Attst (%leyst;)\%esa>

"There, that'll do." Pushing my glasses up the bridge of my nose, I shut down my computer and grabbed my books. I hurried out of my dorm room, heading toward the science building.

Late for class. Again. Why was my brain always three gigabytes behind where it should be?

At 8:30 in the morning, vehicles jammed the parking lot. Fast-forward fourteen hours and the spaces would be empty; everybody would be out partying, having fun. Except me.

I made my way across campus, cutting through the university's parking lot. I noticed a black four-door car pulling into the lot. Despite the tinted windows, I could see four shadowy figures inside. The car circled around the loop, slowing to a crawl. There were no parking spaces available.

What are they doing? Sightseeing?

Cutting across a row, I peeked over my shoulder. The dark car rounded the corner into my lane. I picked up my walking pace, my ears tuned to the engine behind me.

Why don't they pass me?

I zigzagged across another row, and the car sped up and followed. I swallowed, my heart ping-ponging irregularly, and started to run. The driver gassed the engine and came to a stop beside me, blocking my way.

All four doors opened, and I froze in place. Dressed in suits, three men and a woman stepped out.

"Miss Kelly James?" the woman asked.

Hugging my books to my chest, I gave a jerky nod, unable to do much else.

The woman pulled out a gold badge. "You're under arrest for threatening homeland security and suspected terrorism."

One of the men spun me around and pushed me up against the car. My books scattered on the pavement as he grabbed my arms and pulled them back.

The woman patted her hands down my body. "You have the right to remain silent . . ."

Her voice trailed to a faraway mute.

I can't believe this is happening. This must be a mistake!

TWO

I stared at my clasped hands on the table in front of me. I'd chewed my thumbnails down to the quick. I hadn't bitten my fingernails in years, not since I took up lollipops. Speaking of which, I would gladly give a few of my 191 IQ points for a watermelon-flavored one right now.

I peered up at the blurry clock and realized I still wore my reading glasses. Never could remember to take them off. Shoving them on top of my head, I read the time.

9:34.

I'd been in this overly warm, white-walled interrogation room with its stale coffee odor for exactly thirty-one minutes. It seemed more like hours.

Only a metal desk and three noncushioned chairs occupied the center of the room. I'd seen enough TV to know the wall-length mirror in front of me was two-way.

How could I have been so stupid?

Stupid. Stupid. Stupid.

And all for a guy. David. A hot guy. But still.

Lifting my head, I stared at my reflection. I looked tired. Worn out. Stressed. All those words popped into my mind as I studied my limp blond ponytail, pale face, and the dark shadows under my eyes.

Were people staring back at me? Talking? Discussing what I'd done?

I would tell them what they wanted to know. But no one had asked me any questions. They drove me in silence to the police station, escorted me in, sat me down in this room, and told me they'd be back. That had been thirty-one minutes ago.

9:36.

Correction, thirty-three minutes ago.

My mind shifted to David.

David. David. David. Until moving into the dorm two months ago, I hadn't realized guys existed. Well, I realized, just not *realized*.

He was popular at East Iowa University: He played baseball, was in a fraternity, and worked in the admissions office.

Not popular enough for me to go to jail for him, though.

His words came back to me as I closed my eyes. *I'm adopted and my parents are hiding it from me.* The way he'd said it, his urgency, made me go all mushy and decide to help. It's just . . . well, he'd been so nice to me. Before him, no one had ever taken the time to get to know me.

I found some papers. Letters from a man named Mike Share, saying if anything ever happened to him, the man I know as my father would raise his baby boy. I found an adoption document with a government seal and Top Secret stamped on it. It had my name, my father's name, and Mike Share's name. When I turned eighteen I did some research, but the State Department told me I wasn't adopted. Something's going on, and I need to figure it out.

Two men. David's adoptive father. David's real father,

Mike Share. They corresponded. Were they friends? Associates? Mike Share must have known something would happen to him. Why else would he ask another man to raise his son? Government agency. Top Secret. Could Mike Share have been a spy? A double agent? Maybe he's still alive and deep undercover. Maybe he's dead, and the government was responsible, therefore they're hiding his records. Lots of questions. No answers.

I thought I could get the answers by using my computer skills and hacking into the government's computer system.

How wrong I'd been.

Forcing my dry lids open, I checked the time.

10:14.

How long would they leave me here? Hours? Days? Wait. They couldn't leave me here for days. That was illegal. Right?

What would happen to me? Juvenile detention? Prison? Would I be tried as an adult? Oh God, they hung traitors, didn't they?

I covered my face with my hands. *I don't want to die.* Not now. I still had to finish my latest invention, the proto laser tracker, for physics class. And my final in BioChem 440. And . . . and . . . and my keystroke memorization program.

I was about to die, and my geeky experiments were all that worried me.

Jeez.

10:53.

What had upset the government the most—my hacking their system or the information I'd been after? Did I leave a trail?

No. Not possible. I knew how to cover my tracks when entering systems.

11:02.

I shouldn't tell them about David. That would get me, not to mention David, into worse trouble. I should tell them I'd hacked just to hack, to see if I could break their system.

No. That made me sound like a juvenile delinquent.

I blew out a long, confused breath, wanting to get the whole thing over with. If someone would walk in, my mind would stop spinning, and I'd say whatever felt right to say.

12:21.

Oh God, I have to pee.

Someone? Hello?

I'm not a bad kid. I promise. I'm a good kid. I've never done anything wrong. I've never hacked into a system before.

Well, except that one time. My Calculus professor gave me a one hundred for the semester. I changed it to a ninety-eight. After all, it's what I deserved. That was the problem with having such a high IQ. Teachers assumed I was perfect and almost never graded my work.

Did the government know about that? Were they going to charge me for that, too?

12:45.

Please! Someone. Anyone?

Finally, I heard the jangle of keys outside the room. The door opened as if the government had read my mind, and the woman who'd arrested me walked in. She silently took a seat across from me. Then a man entered. I recognized him from the dark car, too. He stayed near the door, standing guard, arms folded over his beefy chest. As if I could escape and run away.

"Where were you last night?" the agent lady asked, placing a notepad and pen on the table.

"The town fair that our university was sponsoring. Celebrating my sixteenth birthday with my friend David."

Agent lady scribbled some words on the pad. "And after that?"

"My dorm room."

"What time did you get to your dorm room?"

Mentally, I calculated when David and I had left the fair. "Ten o'clock."

"What did you do when you got to your dorm room?"

Went to bed, I wanted to say. But I knew they knew I hadn't. Why else would I be here? "Played on my computer."

"How long did you 'play on your computer'?"

"Until six in the morning."

The agent lady looked up from her notepad. "All night long?"

"Yes, ma'am."

"What did you do on your computer?"

I swallowed. "Homework."

"I thought you said you played."

Shoot. "Um, that's what I meant. Homework is playing for me." *Homework is playing for me? Who's gonna believe that?*

The agent lady leveled intense blue eyes on me. "It's going to be a lot easier on you if you cooperate. Now let me ask you again. What did you do on your computer?"

My heart thumped my chest wall. "Hacked into the government's computer system." *Oh God, I'm going to prison for this.*

"What were you looking for?"

Something inside me told me not to tell. David might get brought in, questioned, put in prison. His secret was too important. Something in his past needed to stay there.

"What were you looking for?" the agent lady repeated.

"Nothing. I was just playing around."

"Liar," the agent man spoke quietly.

I jerked my attention to the door where he still stood. "No, sir. I'm not lying."

He strode toward me, keeping his glare pinned on me. I slid down in my chair as he got closer.

He stuck his pockmarked, snarly face right in mine. "Last thing I need this afternoon is to deal with some snot-nosed kid. Now let *me* ask you. What were you looking for?"

My thumping heart pounded so loud it deafened my ears. "N-n-nothing."

Agent man's jaw tightened, then he grabbed my arm and pulled me out of the chair. "I've had enough."

THREE

1:43.

I now sat in a holding cell with cement walls and no windows. The bars to my right looked out onto an empty hallway.

Leaning back, I closed my eyes. How stupid of me to think David was being nice because he liked me. I'd heard the gossip around the dorm.

Kelly's so goofy with those thick glasses, always scurrying around campus in her own little world, bumping into stuff. What a mess.

Well, she's from foster care. They don't really teach those kids good hygiene. David's smart to suck up to her, though. She can do his homework.

Nobody liked me. I was awkward and strange. I knew that about myself.

But why did David pretend to like me? I'd known him two months, and never once had he asked me for help on anything. Had he been cozying up to me, waiting for the right time to drop the government stuff? Knowing I'd hack in for him?

Oooh. What a fool I'd been. That's exactly what he'd done. What an idiot. How could I have fallen for that? He probably didn't even have a government secret. He probably wanted me to show him how to hack, so he could go back later and do illegal stuff.

And to think I had a crush on him. How sad. He thought of me as a sister. At least that's what he said.

Of course that's how he thought of me. He was eighteen; I was sixteen. No eighteen-year-old would actually be interested in someone my age. I was smart enough to understand that.

2:56.

Bouncing my leg, I opened my eyes and glanced at the stainless steel toilet in the corner. No way I'd pee out in the open.

Please! Somebody. Can I go to the bathroom? I promise I won't try to escape.

I had to calm down. Think computer code. That always helped.

<%attrs;--%corears, %il8n, %events>
<Cite<hatru>/Q land="en"-us>
<;IQ ;stng 1-234-5 5</strng>

Okay. Not working. Because my bladder's about to explode!

Blowing out a breath, I ran my gaze over the other occupants in the freezing, dimly lit cell. Four adults.

Straight across from me sat a red-haired woman, her legs crossed, top one swinging, staring at a spot above my head. She wore lots of makeup, a tight tiger-print shirt, and a leather miniskirt. Maybe a prostitute?

A bony, dark-haired woman lay beside her, curled up, sleeping. Bruises dotted her arms, legs, and face. An abuse victim? A drug addict?

In the middle of the stained floor sat an old, gray-haired woman, rocking and crying. She wore a housecoat and slippers and had bed head. She looked like somebody's grandmother. Thirty minutes ago they put her in here, and I wondered nearly every minute since then what she'd done. At first I felt sorry for her with the crying, but now I wished she'd stop. And get off the floor. That's just gross.

A blond woman with a slick, chic bun and wearing an executive suit occupied the same bench as me. She appeared as if she should be working in a high-rise office building. Maybe she'd been arrested for corporate espionage.

Except for the bony, dark-haired, possible drug addict, I'd been here longer than anyone else.

Hours.

Hours had passed since the agent dragged me from the interrogation room and tossed me in here. And my growling stomach confirmed that it was late afternoon.

What was it with these government people? Why did they keep leaving me alone for hours on end? Were they hoping to break down my defenses?

Well, if that was the case, it worked. I never felt so scared in my whole life.

"Hello."

I jumped.

The blond executive woman stuck out her hand. "If I don't talk to somebody, the crying will drive me insane. I'm Connie."

Relief washed over me at the chance for friendly conversation, and I shook her hand. "Kelly."

"Don't you love the smell in here? Nothing like urine and cheap perfume."

I'd been in here for so long, I'd blocked it out. But now

that she brought it to my attention again, it overpowered my senses. "You're awful young to be in here."

"They didn't have a juvenile holding cell."

Connie nodded. "Shall we ask the question on everybody's mind? What are you in here for?"

"Um . . ." I scratched my head, debating if I should tell . . . why not. "I hacked into a computer system." I purposefully left out the government part.

"No kidding?" Connie laughed.

I smiled. "How 'bout you?"

"Prostitution."

I blinked. "Really?" I took in her perfect hair, gray business suit, and expensive spiked heels. "You don't look like a prostitute."

"You don't look like a computer genius."

No, I didn't, and I'd wished my whole life I did. Five-foot-ten. Blond. Blue eyes. C-size boobs. Skinny. *You should model, honey.* How many times had I heard *that* suggestion over the years?

"WOULD YOU SHUT UP?!" the red-haired woman screamed.

Connie and I both jerked to attention.

Red Hair shoved off her bench, stomped over to the old woman, and started shaking her. "SHHHUUUT UUUP!"

The lady let out a wail.

"Leave her alone," Connie warned. "She's just an old crazy woman."

Red Hair turned toward us. She actually bared her teeth like a rabid dog. "You wanna go around with me, fancy?"

Connie shrugged, all nonchalant. "If I have to."

I watched wide-eyed as Red Hair approached us.

"Knock it off." A police lady rapped the bars with a black stick. "Visitor here."

All of us, except for the bony, dark-haired woman who was still sleeping, turned our attention to the hallway outside the cell. A tall, *really* gorgeous man stood staring right at . . .

Me?

Swallowing, I stared back into his light green eyes.

Why's he looking at me?

The police officer unlocked the door. "Back up," she ordered Red Hair.

Red Hair took a few steps back, fists clenched, shooting dirty scowls at everybody.

Police lady motioned for me. "Let's go, little girl. He's here for you."

FOUR

The tall, light-eyed man gave me two minutes to use the bathroom and then took me to an office. No interrogation room this time. No two-way mirror. No big acne-scarred agent standing guard at the door.

Ugly beige carpet covered the floor. It reminded me of the carpeting at my first foster home. A dark wood desk sat centered along the back of the room with two red, cushiony chairs in front of it. Pictures of the beach and the ocean hung from the yellow walls. Vanilla air freshener overpowered the small place.

A few portraits decorated the desk's shiny surface. The man wasn't in any of them.

This office must belong to someone else.

He motioned me to sit in one of the two chairs. He took the other one, right beside me, instead of sitting behind the desk. Like we were equal instead of him being the one in charge.

"Did they feed you?" he asked.

"No, sir."

Lifting the phone, he punched a button. "Miss James hasn't eaten."

Whoever picked up on the other end must have known this man because he didn't identify himself.

"Thank you." He ended the call.

I eyed him carefully. Who was he? What did he want with me? I'd never seen anyone quite like him. Light green eyes, dark skin, and brown curly hair. I'd guess he was around thirty years old.

Hands down, he was the most gorgeous guy I'd ever seen.

He didn't seem to notice me staring as he flipped through a folder. Good thing, because I'd never been so rudely curious in my life.

Should I introduce myself or wait for him to speak? Usually silence didn't bother me, but right now it did. Maybe he was waiting for the food to come.

I focused on the folder he held, curious what kept his interest. As I read the label, I sucked in a surprised breath.

Me?

He didn't try to hide the information. In fact, he held it out as if to give me a better look.

Pictures of me at different ages. School reports. Test scores. Psychological evaluations. Photos of my parents. Seeing them calmed my nervousness. I had a quick flash of my mom pushing me on a swing. It made me smile.

My whole life in one folder. Big deal. I didn't have any deep dark secrets. My parents died in a plane crash when I was six, and I'd been bounced around between foster homes and orphanages ever since.

I continued studying the papers as he sifted through them, and when he finished, I switched my gaze to his. I saw warmth there, and a sense of familiarity. The first time since early this morning I didn't feel like a criminal. I almost felt safe.

He extended his hand. "Thomas Liba."

"Kelly James." I introduced myself, then realized he already knew my name.

The door opened, and an old police officer limped in. He didn't glance at either of us as he put a plastic wrapped sandwich on the desk.

Feeling like a burden, I muttered "thank you" as he limped back out.

Mr. Liba pushed back his chair and crossed the office to a small refrigerator in the corner. He opened it, grabbed a soda, and brought it to me.

"Thanks."

He nodded once.

I unwrapped the sandwich labeled *turkey* and popped the top on the soda can. While he went back to analyzing my file, I ate faster than I'd ever eaten in my whole life. If it wasn't for my hunger, I would've been embarrassed at the chomping and gulping noises I made.

To my horror, I burped when I finished. "Excuse me," I whispered.

"Garbage can's by the door," he said, without looking at me.

Taking that as a hint, I pushed up out of the chair, rounded the armrest, caught my toe on the wooden leg, and toppled into Mr. Liba's lap.

"Oh my God, I'm so sorry." I scrambled off him.

"It's fine," he said calmly, and grasped my arm to help me regain my balance. "Go throw away your garbage."

Quickly, I did, then resumed my seat. *Idiot. I'm such an idiot.* Of all my imperfections, and I have a lot of them, I'd swap my klutziness for pretty much anything.

"I was like you once," he commented as he flipped through my file. "A system kid. Got in a lot of trouble."

Not knowing what to say, I remained quiet.

"Difference is, you haven't gotten into any trouble. Until now."

My throat suddenly went dry.

"You hacked nine levels of the government's main computer system. Know how many there are?"

"No, sir."

"Eighteen. You got halfway there. Farthest anyone's ever gone." He paused and looked at me. "Ever."

No one had hacked farther than me? That couldn't be right. It had been too easy. Their passwords were cleverly coded in the numbers of Pascal's triangle, a basic theory. Such a simple pattern, yet it'd taken me an hour to figure it out. I would've made it through all eighteen given more time.

Mr. Liba closed my folder, but kept it in his lap. "Quite impressive, young lady."

"Thanks," I mumbled, not sure if he'd really given me a compliment.

"I'd like you to tell me what information you were after."

I hesitated, and he patiently waited.

Then I told him everything involving David, the adoption paper, the letter he found, and the government seal.

Mr. Liba listened carefully, his focus glued to me. When I finished, we sat in silence a few minutes as he continued to study me.

"I appreciate you trusting me with the information," he finally responded.

He was right. I did trust him, and I had only just met him. I didn't even know if he worked for the government or not. For all I knew he might be a bad guy, and I'd given away information to the wrong person. But there was something about him that had made me want to talk.

"What I'm about to discuss with you is top secret. You must never repeat any of it to anyone. Never. If you do, there will be repercussions."

There will be repercussions? What the heck did that mean? I wanted to ask, but my heart raced so fast I didn't think I could speak without stuttering.

"I work for the IPNC, Information Protection National Concern. It's a special-operations division of the United States government. I'm in charge of recruiting and training what we at IPNC affectionately term the Specialists."

"The Specialists?" Sounded like the name of an exclusive club.

"The Specialists are a group of young adults. They each excel in one certain area. For you, that would be computers. We take them, house them, train them, give them new identities, and teach them how to one day go deep undercover."

"But wh-what about their parents?"

Mr. Liba tapped my file. "They're all like you. System kids that screwed up somehow. Nobody even knows they're gone."

Somebody would know, I wanted to say, but who was I kidding? Nobody would even miss me. David, maybe, but he'd probably be relieved he didn't have to be nice to me anymore.

"But is this . . . legal?" It couldn't be. Could it? Taking kids, giving them new identities, making them into some sort of secret agents.

"This is all on the up-and-up. I assure you."

"I can't do this. What about my education? I'm supposed to graduate from college this year. I can't go undercover. I'm a total klutz. I get nervous way too easy. I don't work well with others. People don't like me. They think I'm weird. I really won't fit in with th-this group of Specialists. I think you're making a really big mistake here. Wrong person you the picked." I shook my head. "I mean, you've picked the wrong person. See? I can't even talk right."

I stopped my tirade, realizing I'd gotten up from my chair and was pacing around the room.

"Miss James, I understand this is a lot to take in. Let me tell you a few things. First off, your education is at the top of my list. For all my Specialists. It's a requirement, as a matter of fact. No dropouts allowed.

"Second," he continued, "you'll be working from our home base. It's highly unlikely you'll be in the field. That's the beauty of computers. You can tap into them from anywhere. So your klutziness won't be an issue."

He stood, walked behind the desk, and brought out a banged-up blue suitcase. I gave it a quick glance and then another one. It belonged to me.

"And lastly, this is your chance for a family. A place to belong." He walked toward me. "You can either take me up on this offer or go to juvenile detention for your crime. If you choose the latter, you'll never see me again. This offer will never be repeated."

Mr. Liba placed the suitcase on the floor next to me. "I got everything in your dorm room, including your laptop, the drive containing the keystroke memorization program, and the proto laser tracker. Which, by the way, is a very impressive invention."

How did he know the name of my tracker? Stupid question. This man knew everything about me. Probably more than I knew about myself. Wait. He got everything in my room? That meant he grabbed the bras and undies I'd thrown on my bed. I held back a groan. At least they were freshly washed.

"What's it going to be, Miss James? You must make your decision now."

FIVE

I decided to go with Mr. Thomas Liba. Within a day, all the arrangements had been made. In exchange for my new life, my crime disappeared, as did Kelly James. He gave me a new name. Kelly Spree. I had to admit, I liked it better than James, even though it erased all ties I had with my parents.

And I would have to move. But I absolutely refused to get on a plane to California, which would be my new home. My parents lost their lives in a plane crash that I survived. Didn't take a genius to figure out the root of my fear of flying.

To my surprise, Mr. Liba didn't argue. Over the next five days via a bus and a train, I traveled to the city of San Belden in northern California. He didn't join me, said he had another Specialist to see to.

Erin, a girl a little older than me, picked me up at the train station on the morning of the fifth day. She was friendly and talkative on the drive out of the city and into the countryside.

Thirty minutes later, we pulled up to an iron gate. A

wooden plaque engraved with SAN BELDEN RANCH FOR BOYS AND GIRLS hung from the entrance.

Erin pointed to it. "That's our cover in the community. Everybody thinks this a foster home. Nobody knows what really goes on behind our gates and below our grounds."

"Below the grounds?"

"You'll find out soon enough." She smiled mysteriously.

"Are you a Specialist, too?" I should've thought to ask her that sooner.

She punched a code on the visor's remote. "I am. I've been a Specialist for two years."

The gate swung open and we made our way up a long gravel driveway. On both sides of us stretched neatly mowed fields. A standard wooden privacy fence lined the property. Off to the left sat a huge barn with a corral beside it. Beyond it spanned a garden.

Erin circled around the driveway and parked in front of a one-story, sprawling ranch house made of wood and stone. A four-car garage was attached to the side.

"How big is this place?" I asked.

"Hundred acres." She cut the engine. "We're running a little late. Let's go."

Late for what?

Grabbing my suitcase from the backseat, I followed her into the house. A large stone entryway gave way to a wide corridor. A dining hall opened to the left. It looked like a miniature version of a school cafeteria. Its aluminum table and chairs sat empty. Across the hall there was a common area with a big-screen TV, comfy chairs, a pool table, air hockey, and a card table. It sat empty, too.

She led me past a pretty, mountainous mural and down the long hallway. Closed doors, spaced about twenty feet apart, lined both sides. We stopped at the second one on the right.

"There're four dormitory rooms, two for the guys and two for the girls. The adult agents stay in private rooms." Erin took the suitcase from me and opened the door. "This is your room. You'll share it with Sissy and Molly. You'll meet them in a few minutes."

I caught a quick glimpse of twin beds as Erin put down my suitcase and closed the door. I followed her back down the hall to the mountainous mural. She placed her hand on a wall-mounted globe light, and the mural slid to the right, revealing an open elevator.

"Cool," I said.

Erin looked at me and smiled.

We stepped inside and the door slid closed. She punched a series of numbers on the control panel, and the elevator descended. I glanced up at the display. We passed floor one, two, three, and stopped at four.

Erin punched a series of numbers again. "This is Subfloor Four. It's where the conference room is located."

"What's on the other floors?"

"You'll find out when you're supposed to."

The elevator opened into a modern, high-tech work-room. Glass panels boxed in and separated a dozen small offices. Each space had matching black desks, sleek leather chairs, and flat-screen computers. I counted only three people dispersed throughout the workroom. One guy and two girls. The guy talked on a phone. The girls typed on their computers. None of them looked up.

Erin led me around the perimeter of the room and came to a stop at a closed door. She opened it and motioned me inside.

"Have a seat."

I walked into the large windowless room, and she closed the door behind me. A huge flat screen took up the whole back wall, but nothing played on it. Five other teenagers sat around a long, silver, metal table. They all stared at me as I rolled out a leather chair and took a seat. No one said a word as we waited, cautiously checking out one another. I felt sure their brains spun with the same questions as mine.

What's her story?

What's his name?

What illegal thing did she do?

What happened to his parents?

The girl sitting across from me would not stop staring at me. She was one of those Goth girls dressed in all black, with pale skin and a nose ring. Her short, purple hair stood out in all directions. She wore bold black eyeliner and bright red lipstick. The gum in her mouth had to be worn out with the furious way she'd been chomping it.

Made me want a cherry lollipop, actually, to help calm me down.

After a few more minutes, the door opened and Mr. Liba walked in. I expelled a silent, relieved breath at finally seeing a familiar face.

"Good morning. As you all already know, my name is Thomas Liba. My friends and associates call me TL. You may do so if you wish. I am your team leader."

"Does TL stand for Thomas Liba or team leader?" asked Goth Girl.

"Both, I suppose," Mr. Liba answered without skipping a beat. "I'd like to start off by going around the table and having everyone stand and introduce themselves. Molly, please start."

"Hello, my name is Molly Pullman."

She looked like Little Orphan Annie with her red hair

and freckles. Small, too, maybe five feet tall and a hundred pounds. Her T-shirt read "YOU LOOKIN' AT ME?" She sounded so sweet and innocent. What in the world did she do that was so bad?

"Molly," TL continued, "please tell everyone your specialty and why you're here."

She smiled, showing two deep dimples. "Martial arts. I got busted for operating an underground fight club in Chicago."

Goth Girl snorted. "You?"

Molly continued smiling sweetly. "Yes, me."

"Darren," TL interrupted, "go next, please."

"I'm Darren Lightfoot. My specialty is linguistics. I speak sixteen languages. I was taken in for flying in a restricted airspace."

Sixteen languages? Wow. I barely kept English straight in my head. Darren was a Native American with strong features. I'd say he stood a little taller than me, maybe six feet, with a runner's build. Cute guy.

TL motioned with his head to the next.

"Joe Vornes. My specialty is clairvoyance. I can see objects or actions beyond the range of natural vision."

Goth Girl snorted again. "Puh-leeze."

What was it with this girl?

Joe merely gazed at her. Peacefully, as if he was in touch with the moon, the planets, and the stars. "I operated an illegal 1-900 psychic phone line."

To me, Joe seemed better suited as a linebacker. He was big and muscular, and had short blond hair.

TL pointed at Goth Girl to go next.

"Priscilla Ross. Friends call me Sissy."

I held back a laugh. For someone with such a tough atti-tude and look, she sure had a girlie-girl name.

"I'm a chemist," she went on. "Busted for mixing some chemicals I shouldn't have been mixing."

Hmm, sounded pretty vague, like there might be more to it.

"Frankie Board." The guy beside me introduced himself. "I excel in electronics. I was arrested for breaking into museums and banks and dismantling their security systems." He shrugged. "Did it for fun. Never stole anything."

I liked Frankie immediately. With his goatee and arm tattoos, he seemed more suited for riding a Harley than being an electronics specialist. Cute, too.

"Your turn, Kelly," TL prompted.

Everybody's eyes focused on me, and my stomach flopped over.

"Hi, my name's Kelly Ja—Spree, and I'm here because of my computer skills. I system government hacked." *Jeez, I hate when I do that.* I shook my head. "I mean, I hacked into the government's main computer system."

Sissy-the-Goth-chemist snorted. *Again.* "You? You look like you should be a Victoria's Secret model." She turned to TL. "Sure you got the right person here?"

Molly cracked her knuckles, still wearing her sweet smile. "Ya know, *Sissy,* if you don't shut your pie hole, I'll shut it for ya."

And these girls are going to be roommates? Sheesh.

TL calmly put his hand in the air. "Enough. Let me remind you, this is your life now. There is no going back. These people are your family now. Whether you like it or not, you're going to have to learn to live with each other. I am your guardian. I am legally responsible for each of you until you turn eighteen. For some of you, that's two years away. Don't mess with me. Because if you do, you will regret it."

I swallowed hard as he delivered the threat and glanced around the table. Everybody appeared to be as shell-shocked as I felt. Even Sissy, amazingly enough.

"We're going to take a few minutes," TL continued, "and get to know each other, then we'll begin today's lesson."

Frankie turned to me. "So, genius girl, you hacked into the government?"

I smiled. David had called me genius girl, too.

Molly leaned around Frankie. "Genius girl? Hey, we should call you GiGi for short."

Frankie nodded. "I like it."

GiGi? I liked it, too. I already had a nickname and two people who seemed to genuinely like me. Maybe this hadn't been such a bad decision I'd made, giving up my identity and joining these Specialists.

Conversation around me buzzed. I didn't say anything. Didn't trust myself to not sound like a dork. As I listened, my thoughts wandered back to David. Where was he right now? In class? I peeked up at TL and found him staring right at me. His expression softened almost to a slight smile, as if to say, *See, you're fitting in.*

Did TL know the secret in David's past? Would he tell me if he did?

Frankie nudged my arm. "So, do you miss your friends?"

Friends? I almost laughed. I didn't have friends. I had my books, my laptop, my inventions . . . my solitude. I had never fit in. I tested out of eighth grade at age nine, graduated high school at thirteen, and was supposed to graduate college this year. I knew guys my age couldn't relate, but I didn't begrudge them. Adults couldn't relate, either. Most of them treated me like a rare specimen, giving me polite respect.

"So do ya?"

"Sure," I lied.

TL stood up. "Today is Friday. On Monday, all of you, except Kelly—GiGi—will begin attending San Belden High."

I smiled at his use of my new nickname. Funny how it made me feel at home.

"Why doesn't she have to go?" Sissy asked.

"Because GiGi has already completed high school and will be graduating college soon. She'll be attending the University of San Belden."

Not sure how they transferred me midsemester. But they're the IPNC, they could do anything. Right?

TL began walking around the room, placing folders in front of each of us. "Understand that your public education is part of your training. It's socializing; learning to, quite frankly, lie to others about your past, current situation, and future. Each of you will wear a detection device for monitoring. The device resembles a small bandage, but it's woven with a series of wires. Some of the wires serve as GPS—a global positioning system—keeping track of your coordinates. Others serve as audio monitors. Everything you say and do will be recorded."

"You mean even when we take a, um, go to the bathroom, you'll know?" This came from Frankie.

"Correct."

They'll know I'm on the toilet?

TL placed a red file in front of me. "Inside these folders you will find your backstory. Memorize the information. Know it. You will be tested on this two days from now.

You'll also see instructions for using the elevator to this level, Sub Four. And your code names. Each of you has been issued one based on your specialty. You will use these anytime we are communicating while in mission mode. If you choose to use them around the ranch, that is up to you. I encourage you to do so to get used to calling each other by these names. Do *not* use them while in public. Molly, our martial artist, will be Bruiser. Joe, our clairvoyant, is Mystic. Darren, our linguist, will be Parrot. Sissy, our chemist, is Beaker. Frankie, our electrician, will be Wirenut. And Kelly, our computer whiz, was code named Data. But we're going to change that to GiGi."

I smiled. I liked GiGi much better.

Joe/Mystic raised his hand. "TL, how long will we be expected to wear the detection devices?"

Good question, because I really did not want them knowing when I was using the bathroom.

"Until I feel confident you'll do fine without it." A knock on the door interrupted him. He opened it and turned back to us. "Now, I'd like to introduce you to your mentors. They are the original Specialists. Things have gone so well with them that the IPNC decided to do another program. You are the Specialists Team Two."

Erin walked in and smiled at the group. Then a girl strolled in. Nineteen, twenty, maybe twenty-one. A guy followed her, looking like the same age, then another girl. They filed in one by one, all sizes and shapes, much like my own team. Six in all.

The last guy walked in, his dark hair and face partially hidden by the girl in front of him. For some reason, I got this odd queasy feeling. He stepped to the side into plain view and looked straight at me. My stomach did one huge swirl.

David?

SIX

TL nodded to team one. "This is Erin, Piper, Adam, Tina, Curtis, and David. Their code names are in your folders. They are here to get you acclimated to the ranch and answer any questions. Now on to . . ."

I sat through the meeting with the Specialists and TL, but didn't hear a word that was said. With a stoic look on his face, David stood against the wall behind Sissy/Beaker, listening to TL. I wished he had chosen a spot behind me so I wouldn't be distracted by all the staring I was doing. He didn't once glance in my direction and seemed to hang on TL's every word.

My thoughts tumbled forward, backward, and from side to side as I replayed the last two months in my head. David's friendliness, interest, and acceptance. The trust he had placed in me with his adoption secret, if he really even had a secret.

He'd said smart chicks were cool.

What if he really *did* use me for my brains? Manipulating me into hacking the government's system.

And how did TL factor into all this? Making me feel

comfortable, warm, and at ease. Appealing to my sense of family and belonging with the Specialists offer. I'd trusted him.

Recalling everything left me even more confused. If David worked with the Specialists, what had been his assignment at East Iowa University? TL must have known David and I attended the same college. Why hadn't TL told me? What about Mike Share, David's father? True story or not? Was David even his real name? How long had he been a Specialist? What illegal thing had he done to be recruited?

I wanted to groan at the confusion going on in my brain. I felt betrayed and alone again. I *needed* answers.

"That's it for this morning," TL said as he closed his file.

I brought my wandering thoughts back to attention.

"Lunch is in fifteen minutes in the dining hall," he continued. "At one o'clock, we will meet in the barn for our afternoon session. Wear something you don't mind sweating in. We're adjourned. I'll let you all get acquainted."

TL strode from the room, and conversation immediately buzzed around me.

Molly/Bruiser threw her pencil into her folder. "Hey, Erin, what do they usually feed you guys in here?"

Darren/Parrot knocked on the table to get Frankie/Wirenut's attention. "Think we're meeting in the stables to ride horses?"

Mystic raised his hand. "Excuse me, anybody know where the highest point is on the ranch? I need to meditate, and I can only do that on a full moon. And there is a full moon tonight."

Beaker folded her arms. "I'm a vegetarian. If they feed us meat for lunch, I won't eat it."

I chanced one last peek at David. He was deep in conversation with Tina. Jealousy twinged inside me at seeing him speak to another girl. My reaction irritated me. I had no reason to be jealous, and I didn't want to be.

I pushed back from the table and quietly left the room. Not a single person followed me. They were all too busy talking and getting to know one another. I didn't want to seem rude or anything, but I'd never been the socializing type, and I wasn't in the mood to start now.

I made my way around the high-tech workroom, now sitting empty. Down a corridor to the left sat a series of closed doors. I imagined as the days and weeks rolled by I would learn what lay behind them.

Coming to a stop at the elevator, I referenced the instructions in my folder. I punched in my personal code, placed my hand on the fingerprint identification panel, then rode the car four floors up to the ground level.

The elevator opened, and I stepped out. The door disappeared back into the wall, revealing the mountainous mural.

I headed right toward my room. Thank God Bruiser would be one of my roommates. I'd lose a few brain cells if it were only me and the Goth chick, Beaker.

Opening the second door on the right, I walked in. My suitcase sat exactly where Erin had left it. Three twin-size, beige blanketed beds lined the peach-colored walls. A corkboard hung above each bed. I supposed our personal decorations would go there. The one in the middle had a piece of paper tacked to it with my name printed on it. That must be my bed. A four-drawer, white dresser separated each bed from the next. A closet stretched along the back wall. There was plenty of extra space in the long room for at least ten more beds.

In the back corner, another door hung open. I crossed the room and peeked inside. A bathroom with three sinks, three toilet stalls, and three curtained-off showers. It had peach-colored walls like the bedroom, but white tile flooring instead of beige carpet. It reminded me of a smaller version of my college dorm facilities.

Clean and sparse. Just the necessities. It disappointed me a little. I'd hoped it would be homier.

After rummaging through my bag and popping a cherry lollipop into my mouth, I sat on the edge of my bed, pulled my laptop from its case, and cranked it up.

"Not hungry?"

My stomach spun at the sound of David's voice, but I didn't look toward the door. "No," I answered flatly.

"You need to eat. It'll be six o'clock before they serve dinner."

I pulled the lollipop from my mouth and placed it on its wrapper on my dresser. "I'm not hungry."

An awkward moment of silence passed as I pretended to work on my laptop. What did he want?

He cleared his throat. "Feel free to put your clothes away. I'm only saying so because I noticed you never unpacked back at East Iowa."

"I'll get around to it," I fibbed.

I learned a long time ago that unpacking was a waste of time. Things inevitably changed. I averaged a new foster home about every six months, for a variety of reasons: I got too old and didn't match the Klines' "cute little angel" profile; Mrs. Von Harv turned up pregnant and didn't need a foster kid anymore; the Julians thought my blond hair and long legs distracted their precious little Alberto. The list went on and on and on.

David entered my room and sat on the bed beside mine. His cologne floated over me, and I resisted the urge to inhale deeply.

He blew out a long breath. "I know you're mad at me."

No, not really. Confused, yes, and definitely feeling deceived.

"GiGi—"

"Don't call me that," I immediately snapped. Okay, maybe I was a little mad. I'd never been so direct about my feelings until this moment. It felt surprisingly good.

"You were my first solo mission," he blurted out.

I looked away from my laptop and into his brown eyes. I saw compassion there, and sorrow, even though I didn't want to. "What are you talking about?" I couldn't help the edgy tone in my voice.

"TL sent me to East Iowa University for you. I was supposed to befriend you, gain your trust, and get you to hack the government's main computer system."

My heart clanged so hard I couldn't think straight. "I—I —I don't understand."

"I lied to you about my dad. I had to convince you to hack the system so TL could recruit you for the Specialists. It was a test to see if you had the computer skills he thought you did."

A test? "Why didn't he just ask me?"

"To hack the system?"

I nodded.

"Would you have?"

I paused. "No."

"There's the answer to your question."

I stared at David as questions spiraled through my brain, making me even more confused than before. "You said he sent you for me. How did he know about me?"

"That's a question you need to ask him."

"Did he do the same to all the others? Test them?"

David shook his head. "Only you. The others more than

proved their specialties on their own. Got arrested in the process. But you? You wouldn't mess up. You never did anything wrong. TL needed a chance to see your level of expertise, and he needed you to do something wrong because he knew he wanted you on the team."

"So then this assignment to the Specialists in exchange for juvenile detention is a fake. I was set up. I can walk out of here right now and TL can't stop me." Anger boiled inside me as I recalled my arrest.

The way I'd been treated by the agents. Sitting in the freezing jail cell. Deprived of food, water, and a bathroom. For no other reason than that TL wanted me for the Specialists. I'd been manipulated and used.

And David had only pretended to like me.

He reached across the short distance and touched my shoulder, instantly putting warmth there. "I need you to understand you were an assignment for me. At first. But as I got to know you, our friendship became real. I hated lying to you, but I knew it would all come out eventually."

I shrugged off his hand, ignoring the hurt I saw in his reaction. "True friends don't lie to each other. I can't trust you. For all I know, you're lying to me right now."

He nodded, his expression flattening to blankness as he dropped his gaze to his lap. "I understand you're angry." He brought his eyes up to mine. "Please don't leave, though. We truly are a family here. And TL's great. You'll see that if you stick around."

Disregarding the twinge of desire *to* stay, I forged ahead with the questions. "What about you? What's your specialty? Why are you here with the Specialists?"

"I'm sort of a jack of all trades. Know the eighteen levels of the government's system, nine of which hacked through?"

I nodded.

"My dad created those."

Too stunned to do much of anything, I simply stared at him.

"He was abducted ten years ago. One week before my eighth birthday. He's the only person in the world who knows all eighteen levels. He programmed a computer chip with the information shortly before his abduction."

"Where's the chip?"

"Nobody knows. My dad hid it."

"Who kidnapped him?"

David shrugged. "Another unanswered question."

"Is he still alive?"

"I hope so," David whispered.

I wanted to reach out and comfort him, to tell him I understood how it felt to lose a parent, but I stopped myself. For all I knew this might be another lie.

"I grew up here on this ranch. Originally it was a home for boys and girls whose parents worked for the government. A safe house to protect the children of the nation's highest agents. Now it's home base for the Specialists. Local people think it's a foster home."

"What about your mother?"

"Never knew her. She left when I was a baby."

Again, I tapped down the desire to comfort. I didn't know what to believe, who to trust.

"We're all a bunch of homeless kids here," David continued, "everybody for a different reason. We all have unique backgrounds, some with juvie records, some not. The one thing we have in common, though, is our need for a family. We are each other's family." He touched my shoulder again. "Please stay."

I glanced down at my laptop as his heartfelt request

echoed through my ears. Seconds later he quietly got up and left the room. He'd come across just as sincere back at East Iowa University. Always attentive. Checking in on me. Seeming hurt and lost as he lied to my face so I'd hack the government's system.

I'd been lied to before, many times. By social workers appearing to be concerned.

Sweetie, you'll love this house.

Little one, no more moving around.

Darling, this is the last place for you.

I couldn't stay here surrounded by lies and false identities. This wasn't me. I couldn't hurt people on purpose, manipulate them, deceive them.

I pushed off my bed and hurried from the room. I needed to find TL.

SEVEN

With my heart racing, **I** walked across the dining hall straight toward TL. Beside him sat David, but I ignored him and kept my focus steady, concentrating on not tripping. In my peripheral vision, I saw the other Specialists and some adults I assumed were agents glance at me as I passed in front of them. It might have been my imagination, but I swore a hush fell over the room.

TL looked up from his tuna sandwich when I stopped in front of him. "Now's not the time," he responded before I even opened my mouth. "Meet me in my room in five minutes. I'm the first door on the right."

He must have known what I wanted; otherwise he wouldn't have greeted me in that manner. "Yes, sir."

"Why don't you grab a sandwich," suggested David. "Sit and eat with us."

You really expect me to sit here and eat like nothing's happened, I wanted to say, but it wasn't my nature to be so outspoken. "No, thank you. I'm not hungry."

I strode from the dining hall, my heart still racing, and went back to my room. I paced from one end to the next and back again, going over everything in my brain. I checked the clock hanging on the wall at least four times before I made my way to TL's door. I took a quick I-can-do-this breath and knocked.

"Enter."

He sat behind a light wood desk with a computer to his right. Through a cracked door behind him I saw his bedroom. Same colors as mine, except with a blue comforter.

TL indicated I should sit in one of the metal chairs in front of his desk.

He leveled his odd, light gaze on me. "I know why you're here, so I'm not going to waste time pretending otherwise. The IPNC has been keeping tabs on you for years. Anybody with an IQ of a hundred and ninety-one naturally draws attention. Not to mention the compendium computer program you wrote when you were seven years old. It won the National New Mind Award."

I blinked. I'd forgotten all about that program, and the award.

"You're brilliant and incredibly talented with computers. I wanted you for the Specialists Team One, but you were only thirteen. Way too young emotionally to handle your new life. Yes, I sent David for you. Told him to convince you to hack the government's system. I needed it for leverage in bringing you to the Specialists. Based on your psychological profile . . ."

Psychological profile? They had a profile on me? Of course they had a profile on me. This was the IPNC.

" . . . it was evident you would never come to work for me on your own. You're not a risk taker."

"What do you mean you've been keeping tabs on me?" Had they been watching me, following me, filming me?

"Let me assure you we never invaded your personal privacy. We only researched what was public record already. We know your school records, your accomplishments, your test scores. Your family history."

"I can walk out right now, can't I?"

TL nodded. "Yes, you can. It was my hope that once you got here, you would feel at home, find a purpose in life, want to stay." He folded his hands atop his desk and leaned in. "Before you make a decision, I want you to think about these questions: What's waiting for you back in Iowa? Where were you headed? Did you ever feel like you belonged? When was the last time you had a real home, a family? Have you ever done something new, exciting, risky?"

Jeez, he knew the right questions to ask.

He stood. "I'll give you until tomorrow morning to make your decision. It's a big one. Take your time. It will affect the rest of your life."

EIGHT

"What's going on?" Bruiser asked as I entered our room. "I know something's going on. Everybody knows something's going on. Are you leaving? You're leaving, aren't you?"

I lay down on my bed. She and Beaker had both changed clothes, wearing something they didn't mind sweating in, just like TL instructed. I stared at Bruiser a second, amazed at her body. She wore a tight, blue "Wanna Piece of This?" tank top and snug, red shorts. Every muscle stood out in lean definition.

Beaker, on the other hand, still wore her black combat boots, loose black T-shirt, and spiky dog collar. Her long, baggy, black shorts marked the only change in her apparel. All I had was my jeans, T-shirts, and two nightshirts. I owned nothing to get sweaty in.

"Helllooo?" Bruiser waved her hand.

I smiled at her impatient persistence and then told them everything. Why? I wasn't sure. I'd never blabbed to anyone about my thoughts, problems, or issues. I always figured stuff out on my own. But somehow it felt right sharing my circumstances with them. Maybe because they were sort of in the same boat. Except they hadn't been tricked into being here.

Bruiser whistled when I finished. "Yowza. That's some story. TL must want you really bad. He doesn't strike me as the type to do something underhanded. I bet he had a hard time lying to you. David, too. He and TL seem a lot alike. I think I'd be flattered if someone wanted me so bad."

Flattered? Hmm, I hadn't thought of it from that angle.

She pushed up from her bed. "I've only known you for half a day, but this place wouldn't be the same if you left. Right, Beaker?"

I glanced over at her. She sat on the carpet with her back to her bed. She'd had her nose in a book the entire time, chomping on yet another piece of gum. The title read *The Atomic Beta Particle.*

Bruiser nudged her with her tennis shoe. "Hey, I'm talking to you. Answer me."

I almost laughed at Bruiser's boldness.

Beaker shrugged as a response.

Bruiser rolled her eyes. "Pay no attention to her. She has issues. Listen, GiGi, I really want you to stay. And so does everybody else. We were all talking about it at lunch."

They'd discussed me at lunch? In a good way? Usually, people only gossiped about me. Hearing Bruiser say otherwise brought a warm fuzziness to my heart.

She peeked at her watch. "We're supposed to be out at the barn in a few minutes. Coming?"

I nodded. "But I need to use the bathroom first."

"Want me to wait?"

Again, the warm fuzziness. I never had a girl offer such a simple, friendly thing. "No. Go on ahead."

"Yo, Beaker head, coming?"

Beaker lifted her attention from her book. "Beaker head?"

"Yeah, ya know, Beaker. Your chemistry code name."

Beaker's lips twitched in amusement, but it was probably an optical illusion. She didn't strike me as the type to smile at anything.

"I need to finish this chapter."

Bruiser waved as she headed out, leaving me alone with Beaker.

I started for the bathroom, and Beaker closed the book and tossed it onto her bed. I thought she said she needed to finish a chapter.

She stood up, hands on her hips. "So," she asked through gum chews. "You staying or what?"

"I haven't made up my mind yet."

"How long"—*chew, snap, chew*—"TL give you?"

"Until tomorrow morning."

She grunted as a response. "Well, uh, ya know . . ." Then she sort of smirked and shrugged her shoulders, like she was trying to look indifferent but didn't really mean it.

Somewhere between the "well, uh, ya know" and her smirk, I made up my mind.

NINE

I decided to stay. Mainly because the Specialists were such a unique group. I felt compelled to see what types of people they would become, and maybe I was curious to see how I would change, too. And if this place would really turn out to be a home, my new family, like TL and David had said.

When I told TL I was staying, he simply nodded, shook my hand, and said, "Welcome aboard." Not what I'd expected. No smile, no song and dance, no exuberant anything.

So here I stood in the barn with my other teammates. TL, David, and a *gigantic* bald man stood off to the left, talking. The bald man wore a black eye patch. The three of them wore matching camouflage shorts and shirts, resembling a recruitment poster for the military. I tried really hard to ignore their muscles and focus on my surroundings.

Horses were corralled in the back half of the barn, while the front looked like an old-fashioned gym. Three knotted ropes dangled from the ceiling, a bunch of mats were piled in one corner, racks of weights lined the walls, and two punching bags hung from a wooden plank. Huge windows allowed the sun to warm and light the area. Hay and musty horse smells clung to the air.

"Okay, people." TL broke the silence. "It's already after one. GiGi, you were three minutes late. Be prompt next time."

I swallowed. "Yes, sir." Three minutes late? Sheesh.

TL flipped over a white dry eraser board, revealing a list of fighting terms and their definitions. "Welcome to your first PT. We'll do a warm-up, followed by an introduction to martial arts."

I whipped the spiral pad from my back pocket and began taking notes.

Wirenut stuck his hand in the air. "PT?"

Exactly what I wanted to know. Thanks, Wirenut.

"Physical training." TL nodded over his shoulder. "As you can see, this barn doubles as a fitness facility."

Parrot sneezed.

Seeing as how I stood the closest to him, I mumbled, "Bless you."

He sniffed. "Thanks. It's the hay. I'm allergic."

I gave him a "that sucks" face, and he smiled.

"Bruiser," rasped the *gigantic* bald man, squinting in her direction. He beckoned her with a jerk of his head.

I was sure the others thought the same thing as me. *Phew, glad I'm not Bruiser.*

Bruiser stepped out of line and crossed the cement floor to where TL, David, and the bald man stood.

He extended his hand with a big smile. "Jonathan. Nice to meet you."

His oversize grin did not match his appearance or voice, nor did his name. Someone like him should be called Snake or Viper.

Wearing her "Wanna Piece of This?" tank top, Bruiser

returned his handshake with a dimpled, toothy smile. Their size difference reminded me of the David and Goliath story.

Jonathan released her hand and immediately karate-chopped her head.

We all caught a collective breath.

She dropped to a split to dodge the chop, spun around, and kicked the back of his knee. Jonathan landed with a thud on his butt.

Bruiser rolled away and back onto her feet before I had a chance to blink.

Jonathan and TL exchanged knowing nods.

TL motioned with his chin toward us. "That's it for now, Bruiser."

She rejoined our line, all nonchalant, like she hadn't just kicked Goliath's butt.

As we stood in awe of Bruiser's talents, the members of the Specialists Team One filed in through the barn door. They all wore matching black T-shirts with SPECIALISTS printed in white.

Cool shirts. Wonder if we'll get them, too.

The differences between the two teams struck me then. Team One appeared focused, unified, controlled. Team Two stood in a hodgepodge line, each person with his or her own unique style.

Beaker with her nose ring, purple hair, thick eyeliner, and gum chomping. Bruiser with her innocent wide eyes, freckles, and red pigtails. Parrot sniffing and sneezing from his hay allergy. Mystic with his thick neck, blond crew cut, and peaceful aura. Wirenut with his Harley-Davidson T-shirt cut off at the shoulders, tattoos, and goatee.

And me with my little spiral notepad.

Jeez, sometimes I'm a real nerd.

TL cleared his throat, snapping us to attention. "Now

that Team One's here, we'll begin with stretching. Afterward I'll pair you off for your first PT. Understand that although you're each here for your own specialty, fitness is a must. If you're not healthy and able to physically handle the extreme situations you may find yourself in, you'll let your team members down."

Extreme situations? Physical fitness? TL told me I would operate from home base. I was the most uncoordinated, unathletic, klutzy person in the world. Anybody could see that. Otherwise, I wouldn't be standing here in jeans. I'd own athletic wear and have muscle tone.

Okay, I can do this.

Although I really wanted to stick my hand in the air and say, TL, sir, I'm the geeky computer person. May I please be excused from physical training? I have code to key.

But somehow I knew that wouldn't fly.

If this was part of the training, then I would certainly participate.

"Spread out," Jonathan rasped. "Arm's length between you."

Specialists Team One immediately went into position while Team Two sort of shuffled around before we figured it out.

"Arms up." Jonathan raised his. "Stretch. Feel it through your sides and spine."

I'd never been one for stretching and considered myself about as limber as my laptop. But this felt good. I could do this.

"Down. Spread your legs. Work it side to side."

Ooowww . . . my legs weren't meant to be spread this wide. I gritted my teeth and held my breath and hoped for the best.

"Up," Jonathan grunted.

Oh, thank God. I managed to get up and noticed nobody else seemed to be having problems.

Oh, wait . . . a bead of sweat trickled down Beaker's cheek. She glanced over at me and smirked. Somehow it comforted me. I was beginning to like and expect her smirks.

"Roll your neck back." Jonathan demonstrated. "Stop at your shoulders. Up and forward."

David's neck rolling caught my attention, and even though there were twenty feet of cement floor between us, I zeroed in on his muscles as he rolled. Though my brain told me to stop, I couldn't stop my gaze from traveling down his body. How come I never noticed he had so many defined muscles?

"Feet together . . ."

I blinked back to focus and found David staring right at me. I'd never been a blusher, but my face caught on fire. And to make matters worse, a look of sexy intuitiveness creased his eyes.

"Palms to the floor." Jonathan performed the contortionist act.

Feet together and touch my palms to the floor? Is he kidding?

Beside me, Bruiser effortlessly did it, and so I tried. My palms made it to my knees. I gritted my teeth and held my breath and reached for the floor. Gravity or my weight or pure lack of coordination sent me swaying forward, and I landed on my head.

"GiGi, you okay?" Bruiser reached for me.

"I'm fine," I muttered, pushing to my feet.

I did not peek at David because I knew he'd seen the whole thing and was probably shaking his head in disgust. I did look at Beaker and caught her lips twitching. Well, at least I'd amused someone.

We finished stretching, then TL paired each member of Team One with a person from Team Two. As he partnered us up one by one, I slowly realized who I would end up with.

"And, David, you're with GiGi."

I stared at TL a moment wondering why he'd done that. David was the absolute last person I wanted to be around right now. TL had to know that. Was this some kind of test? Part of my overall training? Something along the lines of quickly overcoming and dealing with emotional stress.

With a slight curve to his lips that made my stomach swirl, David crossed the cement floor to where I stood. "Looks like it's gonna be you and me."

"Working with you I'm not." I shook my head, dazed from the smell of his cologne. "I mean, I'm not working with you."

He shrugged. "It's not an option." He picked my notepad off the floor and tossed it a few feet into the corner. "Always taking notes, aren't you?"

Looking over to where it landed, I tightened my jaw. How dare he throw my notepad like an insignificant piece of trash?

"You." I pointed at it. "Go. Pick. That. Up. Right. Now."

"No." He smiled. "I. Won't. Go. Pick. That. Up. Right. Now."

Was he making fun of me? I reared and shoved him hard in the chest, sending him stumbling backward. His jaw dropped in disbelief, and my heart kicked into overdrive.

I can't believe I just did that.

"Hey," TL barked from across the barn. "Save it for the mats."

I peered around the training area and found all eyes on me. Parrot's brows shot up in surprise, as if to say, *Whoa, didn't know you had it in you.* Beaker stopped chomping her gum and stood studying me, like she couldn't quite figure me out.

There was nothing worse than people staring at me. Resisting the urge to run away in embarrassment, I wiped my damp palms on my jeans and made myself stay.

TL began giving instructions, and slowly everyone's focus turned to him. My mortification slipped away. But I didn't hear a word he said as I replayed everything in my mind, over and over and over again. What had I been thinking?

Moments later, everyone grabbed mats and slid them to separate areas in the barn. I followed David's lead because I didn't know what we were supposed to be doing.

David situated our mats in the far corner away from everyone else. He picked up my notepad and handed it to me. "Sorry," he said. "I guess I shouldn't have done that."

I took my spiral pad. "I'm sorry, too, for shoving you."

He nodded, accepting the small truce. "Feel better now?"

"A little." Not really. Because every time I set eyes on him I recalled how nice he'd been to me back at East Iowa University. Under it all he'd been fabricating lie after lie after lie.

"Bet you didn't hear a word TL said."

David knew me too well. "You're right." I extracted my mechanical pencil from the spiral and flipped the cardboard cover over. "Shoot."

"We're practicing basic self-defense today using mixed

martial arts. And how to keep yourself calm during stressful situations." He continued outlining everything while I scribbled notes. Different holds and twists of the body. Breathing. Which body parts you can get to the easiest.

When he finished, I slipped the pad into my back pocket. "Okay, where do we start?"

"Well, first of all," David looked me up and down, "where're your workout clothes?"

"Don't have any. I don't work out."

"We're going to have to buy you some. PT's four times a week. For everyone. You need something other than jeans."

Four times a week?!

"You need shorts."

I shrugged. "Or yoga pants."

If he thought he was getting me in shorts, he had another think coming. I looked *horrible* in shorts. All long, gangly legs like a giraffe or something. Pale, too. Whiter than Beaker, the Goth. Now if I had Bruiser's muscles, I would wear workout clothes anytime.

David circled behind me. "Basic self-defense. You never know what types of situations you'll find yourself in."

He grabbed me around the neck and stomach and yanked me back against him. I sucked in a startled breath.

"What would you do," he whispered against my ear, "if an attacker had you in this hold?"

This was all pretend, make-believe, but the position scared me out of my mind. His tight, constraining grip paralyzed me. I couldn't have moved if I wanted to.

I felt powerless. Helpless. I had no control. And I wanted more than anything to never be in this position again.

"GiGi." TL came up beside us. "Calm your breathing."

I realized I was panting to the point of hyperventilation.

He placed his warm fingers over my face. "Close your eyes . . . concentrate . . . relax . . . center yourself . . . even your breaths."

I did as he quietly instructed. As the moments passed, the sounds of the horses at the back of the barn and the other Specialists muted. I felt only the soft thud of my heart, heard my quiet exhalations. A sense of oneness with myself strengthened me. As if I, too, could take on Goliath and win.

His fingers slid from my face. "Now slowly become aware of your surroundings."

David's arms around my neck and stomach came to me first. In my meditative state, I'd forgotten them. Then his body along the length of mine. His warm breath on my cheek. His pulsing heart against my back.

"Estimate the height and weight of your attacker." I heard TL shift to stand in front of me. "What part of his body can you get to the quickest? What part of your body can you move?"

I opened my eyes, as focused as I was when keying code. "My head. I can move it back. We're around the same height. Head butting is an option."

Head butting? Never thought I'd ever say that, let alone do it. "My left arm. It's pinned, but I can move my hand back and grab his groin. My legs. Both are free. I can slip one between the two of his and knock him off balance."

"Good." TL stepped to the left. "Which option is guaranteed to cause the most pain?"

"His groin, of course."

David quickly released me. "You're right, and TL's sadistic enough to tell you to do it."

TL chuckled. "Nicely done." He slapped David on the

back. "Take it easy on her," he said, then wandered over to another team.

"That was really cool." I turned to David. "I might like this PT stuff after all."

He patted me on the head, making me feel five years old. "We gotta make sure you can take care of yourself. I told you I feel protective. You're like my little sister."

Maybe it was the little-sister comment, the same one he'd made right before tricking me into hacking the government's system. Or maybe the pat on the head. But both gestures infuriated me.

Grabbing his wrist, I twisted his arm behind his back and jammed my foot into the rear of his knee.

He buckled to the floor and rolled to his back. "What the . . . where did you learn that move?"

I stared down at him, amazed I'd done such a Jackie Chan maneuver. *Guess watching movies pays off after all.* I made a dramatic show of dusting my hands, enjoying my momentary superiority as David sat stunned on the floor.

"Excuse me. I need a bathroom break." I strolled away, head up, hoping my rear end looked good. Because maybe then he'd realize I wasn't five years old or his little sister.

TEN

I hurried across the University of San Belden's library plaza and into the computer science building. I'd been attending classes for only a month, but already I liked the professors and students better than Iowa. Everyone seemed more laid-back. Maybe it was the California sun and the surfer attitude.

In the past month, I'd had the same schedule. Classes every day. Homework. PT after that. Dinner. Chores. Bed. Pretty mundane actually. Except I'd always managed to be late to one or more of the various things.

I unlocked the lab reserved for computer science majors and found my usual station in the back empty. There were only two other students, a girl next to my station and a guy in the front. But they were so into their work, they didn't even notice me. With a quick glance at the clock, I put my book bag down. I had two hours until David got out of classes. We were supposed to meet in the parking lot to go pick up my team from the high school.

I cranked up my laptop, laid out a couple of lollipops, and began keying code.

<CTE> [IS0-0000] <ICTE>
<P>=ABR TLE='wowdeb'>ABR<>
<SCE & FER> <003004001> I=~%>

"Hey, there's a *really* cute guy out there who wants you."

I nodded, having heard the student beside me. A few more keystrokes, and this code segment would be complete. . . .

"Um, it looks like it's important. He's pointing to his watch and jabbing his finger in your direction."

I nodded, having heard the girl *again*. Didn't people know it was rude to bother someone when they were working?

The student shook my arm. "He's knocking on the glass now. Who is that? Does he go to school here? Omigod if you don't want him, I'll take him."

Remember to never sit by this idiot again.

Across the computer lab, a blurry image of a tall, dark haired guy occupied the window. I shoved my glasses on top of my head and got a clear shot of David impatiently tapping his watch.

Shoot. I jumped to my feet as my gaze darted to the clock that hung on the wall. *TL's gonna kill me.* Thirty minutes late! How had so much time gone by already?

Tossing my lemon lollipop in the garbage, I signaled David to go on, knowing he'd wait by the ranch's van. Rapidly, I shut down the laptop and raced from the lab, through the computer science building, and out into the parking lot. David stood propped against the van talking to a dark-haired girl.

He's not in such a hurry now.

He glanced up as I approached. "Ah, here she is."

The dark-haired girl gave me a barely discernible once-over, like comparing herself to me. Like she had some sort of territorial right over David.

I wanted to tell her to save her immaturity for someone it actually intimidated.

"Is this where you work?" She pointed to the decal on the van. SAN BELDEN RANCH FOR BOYS AND GIRLS.

"Yes. It's part of my work-study program at school here." He surreptitiously checked his watch.

Dark-haired Girl turned to me. "Aren't you that genius kid that enrolled a few weeks ago? Everyone's been talking about you."

"That's her." David reached toward me, and I got the impression he was going to ruffle my hair or pat me on the head again.

I narrowed my eyes in warning, and he slid my backpack off my shoulder instead.

"Nice meeting you." He opened the passenger side, and I climbed in.

"Can I, um, give you my number?" the girl asked David.

Jealousy tingled inside me, but I busied myself putting on my seat belt, pretending everything was cool.

David turned to the dark-haired girl, and I imagined his mind clicking out of task mode into normal eighteen-year-old mode.

"Oh, sure. Sorry. My mind's on something else."

The girl scribbled her number on a scrap of paper and tucked it down his front jeans pocket. "Call me."

I stared out my open window at his front pocket, unable to comprehend such a bold move. I could never do that.

David cleared his throat and circled around to the driver's side. He returned her wave through the window as we pulled out of the parking lot.

"TL's going to be really pissed," David snapped, after we turned onto the main street.

It took me a second to register how upset he sounded. "I'm sorry. I wa—"

He sliced the air with his hand, and I blinked in astonishment. "Your life's no longer just about you. There're other people involved. Do you realize your teammates have been waiting at the high school for nearly forty-five minutes to be picked up? How do you think they feel standing out there doing nothing?"

I swallowed a lump of guilt.

"They probably think we're not showing. They probably already called TL."

"I'm sor—"

"You can't get lost in your own computer world anymore. There are people who depend on you."

My guilt morphed to anger. How dare he accuse me of not being dependable. Anybody, *anybody*, could depend on me. "Well, you didn't seem to mind my being late. What were you doing with that girl? Tricking another unsuspecting teenager into committing a crime?"

He shot a lethal glare in my direction, and I turned away. Silence filled the air between us as we drove through the city.

Warm air flowed in my open window. Outside, kids played in shaded parks, people bustled in and out of air-conditioned buildings, joggers and Roller Bladers spotted the sunny sidewalks. Everyone enjoying a normal afternoon. A normal life. I caught sight of a family picnicking and immediately recalled a picnic I'd gone on with my parents. The unexpected memory brought a slight smile to my lips. I missed them so much.

I sighed. I had to admit, I had "tardy" issues. Never

could be anywhere on time. Not even alarm clocks kept me on track. Most of the time I tuned them out when they went off. It wasn't as if I didn't comprehend my flaws. I found it very hard to pull myself from my concentrated state. That's all. Something I needed to work on, but I didn't need David barking at me about it.

"Here," he murmured, and handed me an apple. "I know you forgot to eat."

Food. Right. I knew something had slipped my mind today. I took the fruit, and my fingers brushed his. The contact brought our eyes together for a brief second, then he switched his attention back to the road.

I looked at the apple and thought, *How can I stay mad at him?* Mere minutes ago we'd been in a fiery debate and yet he'd still worried about my welfare.

"Ohhh," he groaned, pulling into the high school parking lot. "I don't need this right now."

In front of the school, every one of my teammates was slinging punches in a street brawl. Beaker was rolling around on the pavement with another girl. Wirenut punched a guy in the face. Parrot charged a different guy. Bruiser leaped into the air, delivering a split kick to a girl and a guy. And Mystic, always at one with the universe, stood in the middle of it all trying to keep the peace.

ELEVEN

TL folded his arms across his chest and stared hard at each of us. "I am extremely disappointed. I don't think this is amusing in the least."

Sitting around the conference table four levels beneath the ranch, my teammates and I guiltily dropped our heads. No one had said a word since coming home from San Belden High, so I didn't know what had caused the fight. My curiosity was about to burst one of my brain cells, though. Especially with the bumps and scrapes everyone was sporting.

"You've been here only a month and already I've been contacted by the principal three times. First, because of Beaker's explosion in the chemistry lab. Second, because of Mystic's palm reading in between classes, and now this. I didn't bring you here to resume your juvenile antics. I recruited you because you're the best and I saw potential. But let me say something: as easily as I brought you here, I can transport you right back out. So if you're thinking you're too talented for me to get rid of, then think again. I don't have the time or inclination to deal with behavioral issues.

There is a whole list of other candidates on my desk as we speak."

TL circled the table and stopped behind Wirenut. "Tell me, what was the fight about?"

Why would TL ask that question? We all wore monitoring devices. TL knew the answer. Maybe it was a test to see if Wirenut would lie or tell the truth. Maybe TL thought Wirenut had forgotten about the monitoring device. They were easy to forget, being almost invisible. The only time I remembered mine was when I undressed.

"I will not repeat my question."

Swollen-eyed, Wirenut cast a quick glance toward Parrot as if silently asking if he should tell.

"Sir." Parrot raised his hand, displaying an oozing scrape on his forearm. "May I answer the question?"

TL raised one brow.

"The fight was about me."

"Go on."

Parrot straightened in his chair and inhaled a deep breath, like he dreaded giving his explanation. "This guy was making fun of my Native American heritage. I threw the first punch, sir. I'm sorry. I let my temper get the best of me."

"And your teammates? How did they get involved?"

"They jumped in when too many students ganged up on me."

"I see." TL circled the table, returning to his original spot. He looked at Mystic. "Your principal said you were the only one not involved. Why is that?"

"I don't believe in violence." Mystic gently patted his heart. "Peace."

Beside me, Beaker snorted.

TL slammed his fist on the table, and we all jumped.

"Let me repeat. I don't find this amusing. Or"—he glanced at Mystic—"peaceful. This situation is just the type of thing that would make the IPNC pull our funding. And then where would you all be?" He paused for a second. "You've lost all free-time privileges for two weeks. Every one of you. This is a team, so the whole team suffers. You will go to school, come back, do chores, PT, eat, homework, and go to bed. Weekends are mine, too. Don't even *think* about violating these restrictions. Because if you do, I will, *guaranteed,* put you in juvie hall where you belong."

He pinned each of us with a light-eyed, icy stare. "Dismissed."

I followed my teammates from the conference room, around the high-tech work area, past all the locked doors, and then into the elevator. No one said a word as we rode it four floors up to the ranch level. We exited, the guys went to their room, and we girls went to ours.

Bruiser gingerly lowered herself to her bed. She raised her REDHEADS ROCK! T-shirt and carefully examined the bruises on her side. "Sucks having TL mad at us."

"Who cares?" Beaker flopped across her mattress.

"When exactly did you develop such a bad attitude?" Bruiser smoothed down her shirt. "Have you always been this way? Or did you wake up one morning and decide, 'Hey, I think I'll be the world's biggest crab.'"

Beaker flipped Bruiser off with a black-tipped finger. I held my breath, sure Bruiser would physically retaliate, and I'd be the one to have to break it up.

"Ya know," Bruiser pressed on, apparently unfazed by Beaker's middle finger, "just because your life sucks doesn't mean you can be nasty to the rest of us. Not like any of us have had rosy ones ourselves. You don't see us all sour moody. Get over yourself."

Beaker rolled onto her side, giving us her back. Runs and holes, remnants of the fight, zigzagged her black fishnet leggings. She'd bleached her choppy hair white in the past week. Very different from the purple it had originally been. I experienced a pang of sorrow for her. She seemed so . . . lost.

We all did, but she seemed helpless.

I glanced over to my bed. On my pillow sat a small, red plastic bag. I crossed the room and peeked inside. Clothes? I reached in and pulled out two pairs of shorts, one yellow and one gray. I held them up and eyeballed their extreme shortness. *We're going to have to buy you some shorts.* David's comment came back to me. Had he bought me these? My stomach swirled at the image of me poured into them. Had David conjured a similar one?

Bruiser went to her dresser and pulled open the top drawer. She took off her T-shirt, grabbed an Ace bandage, and began wrapping it around her ribs. "Should've bought a bigger size. Those'll crawl up your crack. They're a little teeny."

They *were* teeny. *Very* teeny. She assumed I'd bought them for myself. Fine by me. Last thing I needed was my teammates teasing me about David or thinking I got special treatment.

"Need any help?" I offered, purposefully changing the subject.

"Nah. I've done this plenty over the years."

I shoved the shorts back in the bag and made myself comfortable against my headboard. "Anything broken?"

"Only bruised."

"How do you know?"

"Ever had a broken rib?"

I shook my head.

"Believe me, there's a huge difference between a broken rib and a bruised one."

Parrot, Wirenut, and Mystic opened our door and strode into our room without knocking. "Can we come in?"

"Sure." Bruiser nodded them in, obviously not caring that she was wearing only her white cotton sports bra and jeans.

Out of all the space in the room, the guys crowded onto our beds like a big, comfortable family.

Parrot plopped across the foot of my bed. He'd bandaged his oozing forearm.

Mystic settled on the carpet cross-legged, like he was about to meditate. How did he get his big burly body in that limber position?

Wirenut pushed Beaker's feet aside and made himself comfortable next to her. She didn't move, and in fact kept her back to us all. He peeled a banana and took a bite.

We were like brothers and sisters hanging out. A real family. With a smile, I snuggled down into my freshly washed pillow.

Bruiser secured the Ace bandage with two metal clasps, then slid her shirt back on. She sprawled on her stomach across her mattress. "I was telling them how much it sucks having TL mad at us. And you"—she bopped Mystic in the back of the head—"are an idiot. I can't believe you said, 'I don't believe in violence.'"

Mystic rubbed the back of his head. "I don't. Besides, if Parrot here would learn to deal with his stress quietly, none of this would've happened. 'Sticks and stones will break my bones, but names can never harm me.' All of you could take a lesson from that. You can't go throwing punches when somebody mouths off."

Wirenut threw his banana peel at Mystic. "Shut up,

man. You got it backward. You need to learn to get physical. Parrot did the right thing defending himself. Nothing wrong with standing up for yourself. If you weren't so busy becoming one with the stars, you'd see that."

Mystic steepled his fingers and pressed them to his lips. "If that's the way you feel, then I thank you for verbalizing it and not violently expressing it." Silently, he contemplated Wirenut. "Harmony lives in my soul. It should live in yours, too."

Bruiser shoved his head again. "Mystic, you're about to snap my last nerve. You look like you could hold your own in a brawl. You should've dug in."

Beaker snorted, and we all turned to look at her back. A second later short bursts of air jerked her shoulders. I smiled at her obvious ploy to control her giggles. The more she tried to hold it in the bigger I grinned.

My teammates began chuckling and slowly Beaker gave in to laughter that shook her whole body. She didn't stop and instead got louder and louder. She rolled onto her back, holding her stomach. Tears sent black eyeliner streaking down her cheeks. I glanced around at my teammates, who were getting as loud as Beaker. Their infectious laughter made me join in.

A clearing throat drew our attention to the door, and we all stopped goofing around. David shook his head. "Such children. You're having too much fun for guys who just got grounded." Bruiser snatched her pillow and flung it across the room toward the door.

David dodged it and charged. He tackled her onto my bed. "You little squirt."

I moved to get out of the way, but they rolled right into me and pinned me against the headboard.

"Uncle," Bruiser squealed. "Uncle. You win."

Laughing, David pushed up and held his hand out to me. "Come on. TL wants to see you at eighteen hundred hours."

Huh?

Mentally, I converted to real time. Six p.m. I glanced at my bedside clock. "That's in five minutes."

"I know. Let's go."

Ignoring David's hand, I rolled off the bed.

"Oooh," my teammates teased. "GiGi's in trouble. GiGi's in trouble."

I waved them off, enjoying the warmth their attention brought me.

David and I left my bedroom. I knocked on TL's door, and David stopped me. "TL's in the conference room."

"Oh. Am I in trouble or something?"

"Or something."

What the heck did that mean? I rewound my brain through the past month, searching for anything I'd done wrong. I'd been late to PT numerous times, and to dinner, and for chores, and I was late today meeting David. If there was anything TL wanted to discuss with me, it'd have to be that. Or maybe he wanted to tell me I needed to wear shorts during PT. Inwardly, I groaned.

David led the way down the hall toward the mountainous mural and hidden elevator. I tried really hard not to stare at his butt, but didn't succeed. He placed his left hand over the wall-mounted globe light, and the door slid open. According to the introduction folder TL had given all of us, a red laser housed within the globe scanned for prints.

Come to think of it, that signal would be much more effective if it were transparent. The red tone gave it away anyway. I whipped out my spiral pad and made a note to experiment with particle beams and quark energy, then stepped inside.

The door closed and down we went. Suddenly I realized I was alone with David. In an elevator. *Alone.* Going four levels beneath the earth's surface. *Alone.* With David. Okay, I'd been alone with him earlier, but that had been in the van, and we'd been driving through town.

This was different. Enclosed. Private.

I swallowed, and the gurgle echoed through my ears. Had he heard it, too? Shouldn't there be music in an elevator to mask all the other noises?

I moved only my eyes to the right. He stood a fraction of a foot behind me. He exhaled a breath and it ricocheted through my brain. The air-conditioning kicked on, sending his cologne shooting up my nostrils. They flared in immediate response. My heart kicked into light speed, and my head whirred on a dizzying wave. I squeezed my eyes shut and concentrated on breathing, like TL had taught me. Slow, even breaths. Block out my surroundings. Inhale through the nose. Exhale through the mouth. Inhale through nose. Exhale through mouth.

The air around me stirred, and my eyes flew open. David reached past me to my right. I caught my breath as I studied his tan muscles. The soft, dark hair. The veins trailing his arm. I followed the length of it to his fingers and watched him key in the code to exit to Sub Four.

I realized then that the elevator had stopped, and because I hadn't moved, David had no other choice *but* to key in the code. How long had I been standing here not moving? Had David said anything to me? Ooohhh, I must look like a complete idiot.

"Sorry, I was proton spread analyzing the." I shook my head. "I mean, I was analyzing the spread of a proton." I chanced a quick peek over my shoulder to see if he'd bought it and nearly ran straight into his face. My gaze focused on a small cut dissecting his lower lip.

He shifted so my eyes met dark ones, and they crinkled sexily as if to say he knew something he wasn't supposed to know. "Right. Did you get those shorts?"

I stumbled from the elevator. "Uh, yeah. Thanks."

"You going to wear them for tomorrow's PT?"

"They're a little . . . teeny."

"Teeny?"

"Yeah, they're teeny."

"Receipt's in the bag if you want to exchange them. You need shorts, though. So don't think you're getting out of this."

"Fine," I muttered, and strode toward the conference room with David close behind me.

"Tell TL I'll be there in a sec." He motioned me on.

David would be joining us? Why?

He headed down the hall with all the locked doors, stopping at the first one on the left. He keyed in a code and stepped through. I swayed to the right, trying to get a look in the room, but the door automatically shut too quickly.

Shoot.

"GiGi?"

I spun to see TL standing outside the conference room. Had he seen me being nosy?

"Let's go. You'll know what's behind those doors soon enough."

Okay, so he *had* seen me being nosy. "David said to tell you he'd be a second. Sir, am I in trouble?"

"Did you do something to warrant being in trouble?"

I hated when people answered questions with questions. "Um, I don't think so."

"You either know or you don't know. So which is it? Be decisive, GiGi. Yes or no?"

"Yes, sir."

He opened the conference-room door and we both entered and took seats.

"Tell me why you answered yes."

"I know I've been having a problem being on time."

TL nodded. "If you'd been prompt today, your team-mates wouldn't have gotten into a fight."

Wait a minute. This was my fault? Uh-uh. I didn't agree with that at all. "Sir, I don't want to be disrespectful, but you can't blame me for the fight. My running late doesn't give my teammates an excuse to get into trouble."

TL smiled. "Quite right. And I applaud you for standing up for yourself. The old GiGi would've silently accepted the blame. You've grown in the month you've been here."

Jeez, he was right. The old me *would* have quietly accepted the blame. I sat up straighter, feeling a surge of pride.

"However, it doesn't excuse your lack of time concept. Let me make it very clear: you'd better figure it out. Wear some sort of watch with an alarm if need be. Brilliance is no excuse to be scatterbrained."

"Yes, sir."

TL pulled a small, brown cardboard box from his front pants pocket and opened it. "Place your monitoring device in here." My stomach swooped to my feet. "Sir?" Everyone else still wore theirs. Why take mine?

"Take off your monitoring device and place it in this box." Panic slammed my heart into my chest wall. Did this mean he was kicking me out of the Specialists? Because I couldn't keep track of time? But I didn't want to leave. Not anymore. I was really starting to feel like I belonged here. Like I was finally part of a family. I almost even unpacked my things last night.

"GiGi, everything's fine," he assured me, as if reading my thoughts. "Take it off and then I'll explain."

I pushed back from the table and rotated away. Lifting my shirt, I undid my jeans and peeled the flesh-toned device from my lower stomach. I didn't know who had created these, but they were ingenious.

If anybody outside the ranch had seen it, I was supposed to tell them it was a wart-remover strip. All of us Specialists had different explanations. Bandage. Nicotine patch. Scar treatment. Of course, no one except my room-mates had seen my lower stomach in the past month, so it hadn't been an issue.

After putting my clothes back together, I dropped the device in the box.

TL put the lid on it. "You are the first in your team to remove the device. I suggest you keep this to yourself. If the others find out, it might spark some jealousy or resentment. As you know, I monitor each of you closely. From the start, you proved to be adept at your cover. You went about your day-to-day activities smoothly, naturally, and without a second thought. It's almost as if you've been here months instead of a few weeks. I'm impressed with how seamlessly you merged into this world. This tells me you are ready to move on to the next stage of your training." He stood. "Follow me."

I trailed behind TL, hardly breathing, thinking, or blinking. The things he'd told me—I couldn't wrap my brain around them. I was the first to prove adeptness? That couldn't be right. I hadn't done anything different from usual. At least I didn't think I had. Most days consisted of a jumbled haze, just like always, full of computer code, with my brain clicking away at the latest challenge.

TL stopped at a silver metal door with a control panel attached to the wall. "You're granted access to this room now. Starting tonight, you'll spend one hour each evening in here with Chapling. He's our computer specialist. Your code is the formula for the nth term of a geometric sequence. You may change it if you like, but please inform me if you do. Never give your code to anyone. Not even Chapling."

TL stepped to the side. He nodded to the keypad. Not a typical numbered keypad. This one contained coefficients, variables, powers, geometric shapes, and inequality symbols. Like a scientific calculator.

Quickly recalling the formula, I keyed it in. The door opened to reveal a computer lab I estimated at thirty by thirty. The coppery scent of solder hung on the warm air. Computers trailed along one wall, various components and tools were scattered on a worktable in the center, shelves lined another wall packed full of cables and assorted hardware.

The urge to touch and explore nearly overwhelmed me. I swallowed the excitement bubbling inside me and wished for a lollipop so I could get down to work. Then I caught sight of a TZ-60 system and sucked in a breath.

TL chuckled. "You'll have plenty of time to explore this room tonight."

I pointed across the room. "A TZ-60. Do you have *any* idea how rare those are?"

"Unfortunately, no. That's your and Chapling's area of expertise."

Mine and Chapling's. I liked the sound of that. Not Chapling's. But *mine* and Chapling's.

"Yo. Did I hear voices?"

TL and I glanced to the right. A red-haired man crawled from behind a patch panel. With the number of cables it contained, I assumed it must control the ranch's entire computer system. He stood and cracked his neck, rolled his shoulders, and shook out his hands. He looked up at me and smiled. I'd never seen such a small adult in my whole life. He stood maybe four feet tall. And I'd never seen such fire-red, Brillo-pad hair.

He waddled toward us, shook TL's hand, then reached for mine. "You're the computer genius, huh? Boyohboy-ohboy. You and I will make quite the team. Beauty and the shorty."

Laughing, I shook his small, dry, rough hand. He was right. We *were* exact opposites.

Chapling teetered over to a high metal stool—a stool I could have simply slid my hip onto—and climbed up. "What time you gonna be here tonight? 'Round eight?"

I had no idea. I looked to TL, and he nodded. "Eight sounds good."

"All right." Chapling clapped his hands. "See you then. Bring the caffeine. It'll be a late one."

TL shook his finger. "Not too late. She's got a morning class."

"Bring the caffeine anyway." Chapling snapped his pudgy fingers. "I'm gonna need it."

TL steered me toward the door. "Chapling never sleeps. He runs on caffeine. If not for me or David, he'd never leave his cave."

We made our way back to the conference room. David had come in sometime during our absence and sat studying a folder.

He glanced up as we entered. "What'd you think of Chapling?"

David knew I met Chapling? Of course he knew. In the time I'd been here, I'd quickly learned how much a part of things David was. At times it seemed that he and TL shared the leadership role.

I rolled my chair out and sat down. "I like him." I more than liked him. In the few seconds I'd met him, he seemed fun and interesting. I couldn't wait for eight o'clock, as a matter of fact.

TL closed the door and took his seat. "I wanted to introduce you to Chapling, but I called you two down here for another reason." He folded his hands on top of the table, looked at David and then me. "GiGi, in one month, I am sending you on your first mission. And, David, you will accompany her."

TWELVE

My whole body went numb as TL's words slowly settled in. Sending David and me on a mission? Wait, had I heard TL right? I couldn't have heard him right. I switched my gaze to David, and his expression mirrored the shock I felt.

"B-b-but y-you"—I took a breath, and then another —"said you would I home base work." I shook my head. "I mean, you said I would work from home base."

TL calmly nodded. "My exact words were you would most *likely* work from home base."

"What?" Oh my God. *What?* He was playing word games with me?

I was suddenly hot and unable to breathe. I couldn't go on a mission. Was he crazy?

I'm going to be sick. I'm going to throw up all over this conference table.

Pushing away from the table, I swallowed again. "S-sick. I'm going to be sick."

David jumped up and TL motioned him back down. "No, you're not. Calm yourself. Close your eyes. Concentrate on breathing."

I gripped the arms of my chair and stared wide-eyed at him.

TL slowly stood, slid around the table's corner, and placed his hand on my face. Just like he'd done during my first PT. I closed my eyes and concentrated on the warmth and weight of his fingers. Their soapy scent. The white noise of the air conditioner. One second slipped into another. Gradually my sickness faded and my breathing slowed to normal.

He took my left hand between both of his. "I wouldn't be sending you if I didn't have complete confidence in your ability. Always remember that."

Complete confidence in my ability? What *exactly* had I done over the past month to warrant such high praise? Maybe this was some sort of reverse psychology. Maybe he'd said the exact same things to the other Specialists.

Memories of the deceit and manipulation from when I first got here came rushing back. I pulled my hand from between his. "Did you know about this mission when you recruited me?"

"No."

"Your exact words were I would most *likely* work from home base. Did you know I would most *likely* go on a mission?"

TL folded his arms across his chest. "No."

"You really believed I would work from home base?"

"Yes."

He wasn't lying. Somewhere deep inside me, I knew that for sure. Then again David had lied right to my face and I never suspected a thing.

"There's no way I would send you on a mission if it weren't absolutely necessary." TL slid back into his seat.

"As you pointed out, I didn't recruit you to be a field operative. I recruited you to work right here with Chapling."

"Then why are you sending her?"

David's unexpected outburst made me jump. I glanced across the conference table. I'd never seen him so panicked. He always came across as controlled and easy going. Well, except when I was running late.

"Last night Chapling decoded intel from Ushbania, a small country in Eastern Europe." TL leveled a passive stare on David. "Your father is on the market, to be sold to the highest bidder."

Silence.

Seconds stretched to eternity and no one made a sound. I couldn't even hear anyone breathing. TL and David maintained eye contact, but not a single expression passed across their faces. I shouldn't be here. This was too private. But this meant David's dad was alive. Why wasn't David happy? Or crying? Or something? And what did I have to do with any of this?

David moved finally, dropping his head into his hands. He rubbed his face, then peered across the table at me. The emotion flowing from his brown eyes made me catch my breath. And in that moment I knew I'd do anything to reunite him with his dad. I'd do anything to reunite *any* person with their parent.

"Mr. Share"—TL spoke, bringing my and David's attention to him—"is owned by Romanov Schalmosky. Apparently, your father was sold ten years ago to this man. Whoever kidnapped him put a twenty-million-dollar price tag on his head, and Romanov happily paid the money. Mr. Share's intellect is world renowned. The government has been actively looking for him since his disappearance. But Romanov has kept him hidden well. We've had an agent working for Romanov for two years, and not even this agent knew Romanov had Mr. Share."

TL slipped a small, thin remote from his shirt pocket. He pointed it at the screen that stretched along the back wall. A picture of a man appeared. He had white hair and a yellowish tint to his skin. An oxygen tube ran up his nose. "This is a picture of Romanov, taken last year."

"Why have you had an agent working for Romanov?" David asked.

"Because Romanov's got his fingers in a lot of nasty business. He's a known terrorist. We've been keeping tabs on him."

"Why now?" David shrugged. "Why's Romanov selling him?"

"Romanov is dying, and he's going out in a fiery blaze of glory. Both of his sons are dead, so he has no one to leave his empire to. He's selling everything, including Mr. Share, to the highest bidder. And he's giving all his money to an Ushbanian terrorist cell. As I mentioned a second ago, your father's intellect is world renowned. He's created some of the most complex systems in the world, including numerous ones for the United States government. I don't think I have to tell you what it would do to our national security if Mr. Share is sold to the wrong person."

"The wrong person owns him now."

TL held up his hand. "I know. Preliminary reports show that your father has spent the last ten years hacking systems for Romanov and Ushbania, stealing money, making them more rich and powerful. Whatever he's done, we have a chance to stop it now, and we're taking it. We want Mr. Share back."

David nodded his head in my direction. "What's GiGi's part in this?"

Good question. I couldn't wait to hear the answer.

"Romanov owns numerous businesses around the world. Based on the intel Chapling decoded, Romanov has encoded the whereabouts of your father on a microsnipet located in a statue in one of his modeling schools. The microsnipet cannot be removed from the statue. It has to be decoded from its embedded spot. Unfortunately we don't know which statue. Intel is cryptic with that part. Obviously, Chapling would never be allowed in a modeling school, but GiGi? Yes."

I swallowed the bile rising in my throat. Modeling? I couldn't even walk right. I was the *biggest* klutz in the world.

"What do you mean, modeling school?" David shook his head. "What does Romanov have to do with modeling?"

"One of his many businesses. He owns a string of schools across Europe through which he launders money."

"T—T—TL?" Both guys looked at me. "I can't do this. Have you seen me around the ranch? I can't even walk right. I stumble into everything. You've got to pick somebody else. There has to be an agent out there somewhere who can do this job."

David nodded. "She's right. She has no coordination. She tripped on her way out of the elevator not more than thirty minutes ago."

I pointed to David. "See, he agrees."

"Seriously, TL, pick somebody else. How 'bout that agent out of Texas? What's her name . . . ?" David snapped his fingers. "Jani. She's hot. She can pass for a model in a heartbeat."

Wait a minute. Jani's hot? What did he mean *Jani's hot?*

"Pick anybody but GiGi. *Anybody.*"

I narrowed my eyes. Really, I wasn't *that* bad.

"Plus"—David railroaded on—"there's not enough time. A month to get her ready? It would take *a lot* longer than four weeks."

Who did he think he was? I threw my arms across my stomach. How dare he say it would take *a lot* longer. And . . . I could be hot. Even Beaker said I looked like a Victoria's Secret model.

"I'll do it." *Oh, jeez, did I just say that?* Too late now. I showed TL all the determination I could. "I know I can do it."

TL nodded. "David's right. There are numerous agents who could do this. The modeling side, that is. But none of them have the computer skills you do. This isn't something Chapling can hack into. This is a stand-alone device. You must be right there to break the code and retrieve the data."

David leaned forward. "But, T—"

"The decision is final. I've enrolled GiGi in Romanov's Ushbanian modeling school. She starts in thirty days."

David sighed. "Well, why me? You said you were sending both of us in. Don't get me wrong. I want to go. He's my dad. But the logical side of me says I'm too close to the situation. I may not be objective."

Hadn't thought about that. But he had a good point. How admirable to put his dad and this mission ahead of his own desires.

"Before your dad's abduction, he created the eighteen levels of the government's system. GiGi is familiar with nine of those."

I flushed at TL's reference to my hacking crime.

"Mr. Share encoded the eighteen levels on a chip. The location of the chip is unknown. According to the intel Chapling received last night, whoever buys your father gets the chip. I don't have to tell you what could happen if someone gets their hands on the chip and infiltrates our system."

"I understand, but it still doesn't explain why you want to send me."

"Intel revealed that Mr. Share's son is the key to owning the chip." TL leaned forward. "To my knowledge you are his only son. Am I right?"

David barely nodded.

"Whether you know it or not, you're the key."

"My dad never told me anything. If he had I would've divulged it to the government a long time ago."

"Ah, and therein lies the mystery. And that is why you are going. As soon as GiGi decodes the microsnipet and finds his whereabouts, we'll extract him. You'll be right there to unlock the mystery of the chip he hid over a decade ago."

My stomach clenched with worry for David's safety. "Sir, what about David? What's to stop someone from kidnapping him now that word's out he's the key?"

"Very few people know his true identity. Only people with access to top secret IPNC documents know who David is. His secret is safe for now." TL shuffled his papers, quickly perusing them. "We're not sure where this statue and microsnipet are located. GiGi will be the only one with access to the entire school. David, you will travel with her as her photographer. I'll go as her bodyguard, and Jonathan will be her modeling agent. I've arranged for an IPNC agent out of Washington to fly in and run things here at the ranch while I'm gone."

Maybe it was the stress, or the whole mind-blowing situation; was this new life of mine actually real? I didn't know why, but I started laughing and wouldn't stop. Images flashed through my brain. Of giant, eye-patch Jonathan, our

PT instructor, acting like a modeling agent. Of me walking down a runway all pouty-lipped, tripping over a piece of dust. Of David studying me through a viewfinder, clicking pictures.

Of David studying me through a viewfinder, clicking pictures.

Gulp.

My laughter died abruptly. *Shoot.* He *would* be taking pictures of me, wouldn't he? I closed my eyes on a silent groan. I was going to look like a *total* idiot.

TL stood. "Now that GiGi's done releasing her tension, you're both dismissed for dinner."

I opened my eyes, but didn't move. I needed to digest things for a while.

TL left, and David got up. "I don't think any of this is funny." He gathered his things without looking at me. "I don't think it's funny at all."

My stomach sank with his point-blank rebuke. I watched him stride from the room, feeling worse and worse with each step he took. He was right. None of this was funny. His dad had been kidnapped ten years ago, sold to Romanov Schalmosky, and was back up for sale to the highest bidder.

And out of everyone in the IPNC, they'd picked me to decode his whereabouts.

Me.

If I failed, David might never see his dad again.

THIRTEEN

Anticipating my meeting with Chapling had helped redirect my mind from obsessing over my upcoming mission.

A little before eight, I keyed in my code to the computer lab. This meeting with Chapling had been in the front of my brain all afternoon and evening long. I actually checked the clock dozens of times to make sure I wasn't running late.

I opened the lab door and stepped inside. Chapling stood off to the right, making a fresh pot of coffee.

I walked toward him. "Hey."

He jumped, and coffee grounds flew into the air. "Oh boy. Oh-boyohboyohboy." He slammed his hand over his heart. "Warn a guy next time."

I laughed, not bothering to point out that I'd been pretty loud coming in.

Chapling brushed coffee grounds from his red, Brillo-pad hair. He finished loading up the filter and pressed the on button.

I caught sight of the stained coffeemaker and cringed. "When was the last time you cleaned that thing?"

He shrugged and waddled off.

I never claimed to be neat and tidy, but that coffeemaker looked disgusting. A sink sat beside it with paper towels hanging above. I turned off the coffeemaker, tore off a wad of paper towels, wet them in the sink, and cleaned it up. I turned the coffeemaker back on, and while the coffee brewed, I wiped the spilled grounds from the table and floor.

Suddenly I felt like his mother.

"Hey, where are you?" Chapling called from across the lab.

"Cleaning up your mess," I called back.

"Oh, thanks. Thanksthanksthanks. Get over here. I can't wait to show you this."

I threw away the paper towels and found him sitting on the floor in the corner, behind a server, surrounded by wires and tools.

I sat down across from him. "Why are you in the corner?"

"It's comfortable. Here." He gave me a wire. "Wrap this around your finger."

I did. He touched the other end of the wire to a tiny, flat microsnipet. The contact sent a hot zing through my finger, and I jumped.

Chapling scrunched up his bushy red brows. "That hurt?"

"No. It startled me. What are we doing? What is this?"

"It's for your mission. The microsnipet's hidden in a statue. We need to develop a device that'll tell you which statue. Something that'll pick up the specific magnetic field that only microsnipets emit."

I unwrapped the wire from my finger. "But I can't go

around with this on my finger touching wires to statues. That'll be a bit obvious."

"Quite right. I was thinking something silicone-based, nearly invisible."

My heart kicked in. "With a remote sensor?"

"Yeahyeahyeah, that's good." Chapling handed me a well-used spiral notebook. "Take a look at my notes. Tell me what you think."

I flipped over the cover. "So how long have you worked for the IPNC?"

"Fifteen years. They recruited me right after I patched into Miami's mainframe and blacked out the whole city."

"Um . . ." I blinked. "Okay. Want to tell me why?"

He waved his hand. "For the fun of it."

I smiled. Somehow I couldn't picture him being so devious. "Ya know, if you would've used a nesrent bug in the software, the city would've strobed like a nightclub."

Chapling looked up from the soldering iron he held. "Oh, thatsgoodthatsgoodthatsgood. Where were you fifteen years ago? Too bad I'm not a social deviant anymore. We'd totally have to do that to San Belden."

We both laughed, and I began skimming through his notes. . . . I was amazed. His computations were out of this world.

I studied his diagrams, and it hit me. "Silicone-based? How about something mirroring a fingerprint?"

He snapped his fingers. "You got it. Smartgirlsmartgirl." He took his spiral pad, jotted a few notes, and we got down to work.

FOURTEEN

<rbba/a;^{x}%#@>
  <: "'/<eltit> "es">
  <gnal <dO&nedlit> /ekup/>
"GiGi, watch out!"

I snapped out of my computer zone a split second before I ran straight into a wall. I'd been into my modeling training for two weeks and knew I wasn't doing too hot at it.

Bruiser burst out laughing, and Beaker snorted.

"GiGi," my modeling instructor, Audrey, said with a sigh. "You've *got* to concentrate. We have only two weeks left to get you ready. And frankly, you've shown little improvement."

"I know. I'm sorry." *I'm tired,* I wanted to whine. This mission had taken over my life. Between college classes and training after school each day at the ranch, I barely had time to eat, let alone enjoy a lollipop.

Perfect, beautiful, *coordinated* Audrey pointed at me. "One more time. Remember, you're a lady. Not a bull rider. Stand up straight, shoulders back, suck in your stomach, dangle your arms. One foot in front of the other, toe first.

Pop your hip. And smile." She demonstrated down the length of our long room and back.

I paid very close attention, *I promise I did,* and successfully made it all the way down our makeshift runway. With a proud, relieved breath I paused for show, pivoted, and my spike heel buckled beneath me.

Beaker snorted. *Again.*

"If you're so perfect," I snapped at her from my sprawled position, "why don't you get up and do it yourself!"

She shrugged, ran her hand through her newly dyed pink hair, and went back to her homework.

Bruiser rolled off her bed, struck a pose, then exaggeratedly did the model stroll in her FRECKLES FREAKING RULE! T-shirt.

Her goofiness made me smile. Leave it to her to relieve a tense situation.

The instructor held her hand out to me. "Come on. Let's take a break and practice wearing clothes."

How pathetic was it that I had to *practice wearing clothes?*

She'd laid a variety of outfits on my bed. Sequined gowns, slinky dresses, spaghetti-strapped shirts, extremely *teeny* minis. Just as teeny as my shorts (that I still hadn't worn, or taken back. Sweatpants and PT went together *just* fine in my mind.)

I eyeballed the clothes on my bed. Did models actually wear this stuff?

"It's not enough to look good. You have to know you look good. Confidence is the key."

Comfort is the key, I wanted to say, but wisely kept my thoughts to myself. Didn't do me any good to fight the process. I had a mission to get ready for.

The instructor picked up a silver, teeny mini and a tight, pink tank top. "This argentine and salmon are great together."

Argentine and salmon? Why couldn't she just say silver and pink?

She handed me the clothes, and I turned toward the bathroom.

"No. Change here. You'll have no privacy among the other models. You'll be poked and prodded and nipped and tucked. Between the stylists, makeup artists, and designers, you won't be left alone. Start getting used to it. Lose your modesty. Strip."

Even though I'd spent plenty of time in orphanages, foster homes, and college dormitories, I still managed to find privacy.

I looked at Bruiser, then Beaker, and then Audrey. *I don't have anything they don't,* I reassured myself, but mine was mine and theirs was theirs. Know what I mean?

Quickly, I made a mental inventory of my underwear.

Bra: beige, one month old, slightly padded, clean, no holes, no frays.

Underwear: burgundy, bought same time as bra, bikini, clean, no holes, no frays.

Okay, now hair: shaved my pits, legs, and bikini line last night.

Things aren't as bad as they could be.

I stripped from my jeans and T-shirt and reached for my new clothes.

"Where's your patch?" asked Beaker.

Shoot. Forgot about that. I continued dressing as if she'd asked a normal question, like What time is it? "What patch?"

"What patch? The annoying tracking patch we're all

ordered to wear. TL told you to wear yours on your stomach."

I zipped up my skirt while my brain formulated a dozen different responses and my heart raced with the lie I was about to tell. "It gave me a rash. So TL told me to take it off while I'm here at the ranch."

Staring Beaker straight in her bold eyeliner eyes, I showed her a hint of concern mixed with solid honesty. "And yours? It hasn't irritated your skin, has it?"

She shook her pink head but continued to study me like she wasn't quite sure whether or not I'd told her the truth.

I glanced beyond her to Bruiser, who quickly looked away. I got the distinct impression TL had removed her patch as well.

Someone knocked on our door, and I checked my bedside clock in immediate reaction. Ten minutes until my next session. Good. Not running late. I'd developed quite a bit of paranoia over that issue.

"Enter," Bruiser commanded in an obvious attempt at copying TL's voice.

David opened the door, and my whole body immediately warmed. "Not bad, Bruiser."

She grinned. "Thanks."

He switched his attention to me, making my heart kick my ribs. Slowly, he did a once-over, from the top of my head to the toes of my silver heels and back up again. I fought the urge not to cover my gangly legs. At least the tanning bed in town that Audrey made me lie in had taken the ghostly glow from my body.

"Isn't she hot?" Bruiser bounced her brows.

David cleared his throat. "Change of plans. We're all meeting in the barn in ten. Not Chapling's lab." David looked me over once more and then quickly left and closed the door.

"Well, I think you're hot," Bruiser said.

I curved my lips upward, although I really didn't feel like a smile. "Thanks, Bruiser."

She hugged me. "You're going to do fine on this mission. Don't sweat it. Isn't that right, Beaker?"

Beaker sniffed as a response.

Oh, well, at least I had Bruiser's support.

"We're all done here." Audrey began folding my model clothes. "Go ahead and get ready for your next meeting."

I unzipped my skirt, thinking back to David. He could've at least said I looked nice. Then again David hadn't said a whole lot to me in the past two weeks. Not since I broke into laughter at the news that his dad was up for sale. And my gut still guiltily clenched every time I recalled the whole thing.

David had to understand that was a nervous reaction. Did he actually think I'd find something so tragic funny?

Being the social reject I was, I hadn't ventured into the topic with him. And I'd had plenty of opportunities to do so over the past weeks. Maybe the whole thing would magically resolve itself.

Right.

Grow up, GiGi. You need to apologize.

But it felt strange, *me* apologizing to *him*. Ever since I came here he'd been the one in the wrong. Lying to me, tricking me. I hated to admit it but I liked having the upper hand.

And how immature was that?

Ashamed at my shallow thoughts, I changed back into my jeans and T-shirt. If I left right now, I could catch David alone before our next training. Apologize, clear my conscience.

I ran for the door and zipped down the hall to David's room.

Adam, one of his roommates, answered my knock. "Sorry, not here. Check below."

"Thanks." I bolted to the elevator, rode four levels down, and ran to the conference room. Empty. I spun around and sprinted to the hall with all the locked doors. My gaze fell on the one I had seen David go through two weeks ago. No use knocking. No one would answer if I did.

I darted to the computer lab, keyed my code, and stuck my head in. "Chapling?"

Crash. Bang. "Ow! What?"

"Seen David?"

"No."

I peeked at my watch. *Shoot.* Only five minutes until my next training. It wasn't enough time to check the common area. I'd have to apologize to David later.

Chapling waddled out from behind the patch panel rubbing his head. "Come in a little quieter next time. I'm an old man. My heart can't handle your youth."

"You're not that old. You're only thirty-five."

"Old enough to be your father. Fifteen years away from half a century. Factor in pollution, hormones in meat, artificial sweeteners, preservatives, fertilizer, and thermal pulsations emitted from this equipment." He swept his pudgy arm around the room. "And I might die tomorrow."

"How much caffeine have you had?"

"A pot of coffee and some soda."

I narrowed my eyes. "How many sodas?"

He coughed a mumbled answer.

"How many?"

Guilty as ever, he lowered his gaze to the floor. "Six."

"Chaaapliiing . . ." Much like TL and David, I had taken on a guardian role with Chapling. Go figure, me a parent. But he just *couldn't* take care of himself. If it weren't for TL, David, and me, Chapling would probably never eat anything remotely healthy or see the outdoors.

I tapped my watch. "Don't be late." The only person with a worse time problem than me was Chapling. Funny how I, queen of forgetfulness, reminded somebody else to watch the clock.

He waved me off. "Yeahyeahyeah. See ya there."

I strode toward the barn with two minutes to spare, sure I'd be the first one. Or at least the second. Maybe I'd have a chance to talk to David after all. I slid open the metal door, and everyone turned to stare. I double-checked my watch, then cast a quick glance to the clock hanging on the wall. Same time.

TL shaded his eyes from the late-afternoon sun shining in behind me. "Come on in, GiGi."

Gathered around a tall, wooden table stood Jonathan, TL, David, and Wirenut.

TL tapped his finger to the blueprints spread across the table. "These are the plans for the modeling school. Chapling hacked into Romanov's computer system and retrieved them. Wirenut has analyzed them, comparing them to similar buildings and security systems throughout Europe. He's come up with various scenarios GiGi may encounter while inside."

I slipped on my glasses and stepped up next to Wirenut.

He scooted over. "Want me to wait for Chapling?"

"I just saw him. He should be on his way."

Shaking his head, TL unclipped his cell phone from his belt. "I'll text him."

Text him? Oooh, Chapling's in trouble now.

Wirenut swept his hand over the plans. "Okay, here goes. Romanov's modeling school is three stories. Bottom's for shows, middle's where the girls get prepped, top's the offices."

"How 'bout rooms?" I readjusted my glasses. "Where do the models stay?"

TL replaced his cell phone. "It isn't a school in the literal sense. It's for finishing. Where models make their debut. You, Jonathan, David, and I will have a suite at a nearby hotel."

A suite at a nearby hotel? With TL and Jonathan? And David? I'd be the only girl on this trip. I glanced at each of them. They were studying the blueprints, obviously unfazed by the revelation that we would all be living together in very close quarters.

Wirenut drew penciled Xs on various spots over the plans. "My preliminary projections show standard video monitoring throughout. These will include optical sensors, so don't look directly into the cameras. You'll be scanned, ID'd, and entered in their computer system."

"I can extract the info if that mistakenly happens," I said. Probably the easiest thing I *would* do on this mission.

"Two weeks from now you'll be so well trained it won't"—TL accentuated the *t* in *won't*—"mistakenly happen."

O-kay. Nothing like the pressure of perfection to make me feel comfortable.

"Sorrysorrysorry." Chapling suddenly appeared, shuffling in from the back where the horses were corralled. "I'm here. Only a few minutes late. Only a few."

I peered around the barn wondering where he'd come from. Not through the main door like me. Maybe a secret passage? Hidden tunnel? Concealed cave? Or maybe a plain old simple back door. All this spy stuff made my imagination run wild.

David reached under the table and pulled out a stool. Chapling climbed up with a grunt.

TL cupped him on the shoulder. "Don't worry about it. Let's get down to business." He quickly repeated all the earlier information.

Wirenut penciled tick marks on the third floor of the plans. "Let's focus on the offices first. They have the most advanced security. Each door has one of three locking devices—either a kemot semiconductor, spoar OAK, or Bearn pamp. They'll work off various configurations of optonet modes, integrated wireless, and IC sock tubes."

Excitement kicked my heart a beat. I'd never actually seen this stuff, only heard about it. "In addition to optonet modes, doesn't the spoar OAK have a series of automated levilon strobes? They're nonspecified nel fuses working in conjunction with a row of thermal ferrit coders."

"Oooh, oooh." Chapling bounced on his stool. "What if instead of the ferrit coders they had unction sizers and oscilloscope meters? Then we'd get a sort of ENAM closure with ruptible del pipes and voltage suppression istors."

I laughed. "Yeah, but if they had micro murotos, it'd be a xican with vashiy fuses."

Chapling laughed so hard that he snorted. "Oh . . ." He grabbed a handkerchief from his back pocket and wiped his eyes behind his glasses. "That is . . ." Snort, snort, laugh, laugh. "So funny." He slapped his knee. "You kill me. You come up with the funniest stuff."

Until meeting Chapling, I'd never considered myself humorous. But in the weeks I'd known him, I cracked more jokes than I had in probably my whole life. We understood each other on a geeky level.

He took a deep breath. "Oh, goodness. Okay. I'm done now."

We smiled at each other, and I realized TL, David, Jonathan, and Wirenut were all wide-eyed, staring at us.

Welcome to Geek 101.

TL cleared his throat. "Wirenut, please continue."

Ignoring my nerdy embarrassment, I pushed my glasses up and refocused on the modeling school's blueprints.

Wirenut expertly outlined the entire school, including every room, hallway, bathroom, and office. He detailed the latest technology and the different scenarios I might encounter in each room. Everything from motion detectors and infrared video to microphoto recorders and gallium probes.

As I listened to him, it became clear why he'd been recruited by the IPNC. Wirenut, literally, was an electronic genius.

He paused to spread a transparent film over the blueprints. "Now bombs."

Bombs? No one had said anything about bombs.

"It's my opinion," Wirenut forged on, apparently unfazed by my sudden jerk-to-attention, "the microsnipet GiGi will extract will be rigged with explosives."

He went on to describe diode arrays and spectro components. But I barely heard a word, as focused on *bombs* and *explosives* as I was.

"That'll do it." Wirenut unwrapped a candy bar and took a bite. "Whaddaya think?"

TL nodded. "Very well done."

"Thanks."

TL looked across the table at me, and I got this nauseating feeling he was going to put me on the spot. "Repeat back everything Wirenut said."

I swallowed. Why me? Why not David or Jonathan? They were going on the trip, too. And oh, jeez, I totally missed the whole last part.

Taking off my glasses, I cleaned them as my brain clicked everything into order. If I blew my nose, it'd buy me some time, but I didn't have a tissue. I replaced my glasses and looked at everyone. They were all silently watching me. Beside me, Wirenut shifted, putting his shoulder right against mine.

It's silly, but the slight, warm contact brought me such comfort. I took a deep breath, opened my mouth, and spoke. Successfully. I reiterated everything, even the part I thought I'd missed. I only forgot one thing and considered throwing in a DTG module to cover my gap in memory, but chose honesty instead. "I'm sorry. I can't remember the type of discharge tubes used in the last bomb."

"Wow." Chapling rapid-fire clapped. "Is she smart or what?" Smart? I didn't feel so smart. I should've remembered the discharge tubes.

One corner of TL's mouth lifted in a sort of half smile. "Nice job. You're the first person I've ever worked with who has recalled their technology briefing in such detail."

"Oh." And to think I'd been sweating over the identity of a couple of tubes.

"That's a wrap." TL rolled the plans and tucked them beneath his arm. "Dinner in ten."

He strode from the barn, leaving me alone with the rest of the guys.

"I'm impressed," Jonathan rasped, "with you two teenagers. It's comforting to know you're on my side of the law."

Wirenut and I looked at each other with matching cheesy grins. "Thanks," we answered in unison.

Chapling hopped down from his stool. "Gotta get back to work. Gotta get back." He and Jonathan headed toward the door, and right before they exited, Chapling turned back. "You go, girl."

I laughed at his use of slang.

Wirenut put his arm around my shoulder. "Don't worry about anything. You've got this mission in the bag." He gave me a quick squeeze. "Coming to dinner?"

"Be there in a few. And Wirenut?"

"Hmm?"

"I'm really wowed by your knowledge. I wanted you to know."

He waved me off. "It's no big deal."

I doubted that. His shy, evasive expression said my compliment made him proud. My heart got all fuzzy. I suddenly wanted to praise someone else.

Another quick squeeze and he was gone, leaving David and me alone.

"You've made quite an impression on everyone."

His words were flattering, but the tone of his voice didn't match. I missed his warm smile and easy bantering.

"I'm sorry, David, for laughing about your father's situation. I don't know why I laughed. I know you probably think I'm inconsiderate and insensitive, but I don't find anything funny about his kidnapping. And I can't begin to understand what you're going through right now. I have a few wonderful memories of my parents, but that's it. At least I know they're dead." I should. I was right beside them when the plane crashed.

I took off my reading glasses to clear his image. "I've always had closure. But you? You've been in limbo for years.

Not knowing if your dad is dead or alive, being tortured or treated nicely. And now you know he's alive, but there's no guarantee we'll bring him home. I'm so sorry you've gone through those emotions. I promise you I *will* decode his whereabouts from the microsnipet. I won't fail you or the IPNC. And I am so, so sorry I laughed at the situation."

I fell silent. I'd never spoken so much in my life.

David stared at me, expressionless. The more he stared, the slower and deeper my heart thudded. It never occurred to me that he *wouldn't* forgive me. Now I wondered.

He cleared his throat, then swallowed. "Apology accepted." He crossed the cement floor and kept right on going out the open barn door, leaving me standing there alone.

Time heals all wounds. A social worker told me that once. I sure hoped it held true in all situations. Because I couldn't picture my life without David's friendship.

FIFTEEN

One week later I strode into the barn wearing my brand-new gray yoga pants and white sport tank top. I felt a little like Bruiser all decked out in my athletic wear.

The teeny shorts still sat in their bag right where I'd left them almost a month ago.

Adam and Erin from Team One sat on the mats with Beaker and Wirenut, stretching and talking. I went over and joined them.

Jonathan, TL, and David were busy hanging punching bags from the roof beams.

Mystic, Parrot, and Bruiser wandered in a minute or so later. I caught their eyes and tapped my watch. *Ha ha, I'm here before you.* They all made faces at me.

The three of them joined us on the mats, and we continued stretching. I had to admit, this stretching thing felt pretty darn good. It was my favorite part of PT.

"Okay," Jonathan rasped. "Everyone up and over here."

We all filed across the barn to where six punching bags now hung.

"We're going to pair you up two to a bag. We're practicing punches today." Jonathan lined up with a bag and delivered a slow-motion punch. "Notice my left foot is slightly in front of my right. Notice my thumb is tucked down. Watch how my arm rotates slowly halfway there so my fist makes contact with the bag straight on."

In slow motion, he demonstrated a few more times and then sped up as he side-shuffled around the bag.

Okay, I could probably do the slow-motion punch thing. But the lightning-quick, side-shuffle thing? No way.

Jonathan paired me with Erin from Team One.

"You first," I insisted.

She did three slow-motion punches and immediately went into the speedy side-shuffle maneuver, making her way around the bag.

I enviously watched her, hoping, *hoping,* I would do half as well. Of course, she'd been doing this a lot longer than me.

"Switch," Jonathan shouted.

With a sigh, I lined up with the bag. *Here went nothing.* I positioned my left foot slightly in front of the right. Concentrating on my thumb position, I made a fist. In extra-extra-slow motion, I brought it back and then moved it forward, rotating halfway as Jonathan had demonstrated.

My fist barely grazed the bag.

I inched forward a little bit and did the whole thing again, attentive to my form, focusing on the instructions Jonathan had given.

In my peripheral vision, the others were already shuffling around their bags, throwing punches.

I blocked out the fact they were all ahead of me and refocused on my technique.

TL came up beside me. "You're thinking too hard. Just try one. Let your body take over."

Purposefully blanking my brain, I threw a punch. It was a little awkward, but I had to admit, it felt better than the slow-motion ones.

I tried again. Better.

And again. Better.

With each one, my confidence was boosted.

"Good," TL encouraged. "Now shuffle. Don't think. Shuffle."

I side-shuffled around the bag, throwing uncoordinated punches. As the minutes ticked by, my feet and arms developed an in-sync rhythm.

My vision zeroed in on the bag as I continued throwing punches. Sweat trickled down my neck. Adrenaline surged through my veins. I had the unnerving urge to growl or grunt or something equally aggressive.

"Stop," Jonathan commanded.

Breathing heavily, I stepped back and glanced over to David. He gave me a nod of approval, and I smiled.

I felt tougher right now than I had in my whole life. I was ready to kick some bad-guy booty!

SIXTEEN

Four days later, I stepped up onto an actual runway.

My modeling instructor, Audrey, handed up an umbrella to me. "One of the designers you'll be working with always accessorizes with umbrellas. There're only three days left before you leave. You can do this. I *know* you can."

Down the center of the barn ran a long, gleaming wood runway, about four feet off the ground. On both sides sat all the members of Teams One and Two, including TL, Jonathan, and Chapling. Everyone held a camera.

Audrey tapped beside my high heels. "This is an exact replica of the runways you'll be walking down. And they"—she nodded at everyone—"are here to mimic the reporters and photographers. It's important that you don't get distracted by all the flashes that will be going off."

I glanced down the length of the runway. It seemed to stretch for eternity. I ran my gaze over everyone sitting on both sides. They all silently stared back.

Swallowing, I fixed my focus on the barn doors and nodded. "Ready."

Audrey squeezed my ankle. "Smile. Suck in stomach. Shoulders back. And don't forget to pop your hip." She stepped away. "Lights."

The overhead lights went out, sending the barn into darkness. The runway was lit down both sides with a soft yellow glow. Everyone began flashing cameras.

Fighting the urge to squint against the flashes, I took my first step, and then the next, falling into the strut Audrey had taught me. *Smile. Suck in stomach. Shoulders back. Pop hip. Smile. Suck in stomach. Shoulders back. Pop hip.* My slinky blue dress swished against my upper thighs. I felt . . . sexy.

I got to the end and twirled my umbrella (Audrey didn't even tell me to do that). I pivoted and strutted back down the runway. I got to the end, and everyone broke into applause.

And I leaped, literally, for joy. I did it!

SEVENTEEN

"GIGI? GIGI, are you okay?"

Feeling as miserable as a worn-out hard drive, I shuffled past Bruiser and, with a groan, flopped face-first onto my comfy bed.

"What is it? Are you sick? Dude, this is like the worst time ever for you to be sick. You guys leave for Ushbania tomorrow." Bruiser picked up the phone between our beds and punched some numbers. "I'm calling TL. He needs to know you're sick."

I slid my right arm from beneath me and plopped it over the phone, knocking it to the floor. "I don't want TL knowing I got my period."

"Oh." Bruiser picked it up. "That sucks."

Miserably I nodded. I was leaving tomorrow for the most important event in my life, and Mother Nature had decided to give me a farewell party. Perfect. I *loved* being a girl. Beside me I heard Bruiser opening and closing drawers.

She touched my shoulder a few seconds later. "Here. Some muscle relaxers from when I sprained my neck."

Bruiser always had some sort of injury going on.

Gritting against the cramps, I rolled onto my side. Her KICK SOME BOOTY T-shirt greeted me. In her small, outstretched hand lay two horse pills.

"Those prescription?"

She nodded.

"You're not supposed to take other people's prescriptions." Jeez, did I sound like a nerd or what?

Bruiser rolled her green eyes. "You're such a goodygoody. Take 'em already. Not like it's gonna kill you."

I did feel like a goody-goody, always following the rules. Even *I* sometimes annoyed myself. That couldn't be good. "What's the brand name?" I had to at least show some caution.

Bringing them close to her freckled face, she inspected them. "Huh. Whaddaya know? Motrin."

Motrin? A recognizable over-the-counter name. Not canpifretrin, asmopowprin, tyquilnoleny, or some other crazy long word no one ever heard of. "I'll take one. If I need the other, I'll ask you for it." Better to be on the safe side.

"You're so cautious," she teased.

I stuck out my tongue, and we both laughed.

"Hey." David peeked into our open doorway, and my stomach whoopdy-whooped. I saw him every day, but the unexpected sightings did it to me every time. "TL wants to see everyone in the common area."

Tossing the pill in my mouth, I washed it down with hours-old, warm soda.

David walked in. "What are you taking? What's wrong? Is that a pill? Are you sick?"

His concern turned my insides all mushy. It'd been two weeks since my apology to him, and we'd managed to return to a stable friendship. Nothing like before, though. His emotions surrounding his dad made him more serious and focused.

Bruiser held out her hand. "Calm down. No big deal. She got her p—"

"Points taken off my last exam and it, um, gave me a headache. That's right, I have a headache, and Bruiser gave me some pills." I smiled, even though my heart thundered, and I silently prayed that David would *immediately* drop the subject.

His lips curved up knowingly. *Oooh.*

"Be quick about it. TL doesn't like waiting."

As soon as David left, I slung my pillow at Bruiser. "I'm going to kill you," I hissed. "I can't believe you almost told him I'm on the big P."

She laughed. "So what? Not like it's a national secret that women have them."

"Well, no, but—"

"Come on."

I followed Bruiser down the carpeted hall to the common area, where the double doors sat closed. Strange, these doors were never shut. Bruiser and I exchanged curious looks, then she raised her fist and knocked.

"Enter," TL commanded.

She grasped the knob on the right, I took the one on the left, and we both pushed . . .

"Surprise!"

Balloons. Everywhere. Red, white, blue, pink, purple. With multicolored ribbons streaming in curls from each one. And people. Standing and grinning, holding glasses of champagne. Staring at me. All the members of Team One. Jonathan, TL, Chapling, and David. Wirenut, Mystic, Parrot, and the newly dyed, yellow-haired Beaker, who wore her usual smirk.

Bruiser smiled at me as she went to join the crowd. Twerp. She knew about this.

TL brought me a glass. "It's your send-off party. We do one for all first missions."

No one had ever, *ever,* thrown me a party. With a grin I knew split my face in two, I took the glass.

"To GiGi's first mission." TL lifted his champagne. "May her flight over and back and everything in between be successful."

I joined everyone in taking a sip. Wow. Real champagne. Not some sparkling white grape juice. Of course all of us minors had the equivalent of one sip. Hey, one sip's better than nothing.

Wait a minute. Did he say flight over? Of course he said flight over. How *did you think you would get there?* Sail across the ocean? But I didn't fly. TL knew that. I couldn't fly. I absolutely couldn't get on a plane.

I glanced around the room to see if anyone else had noticed the mistake. But they were all talking. Someone cranked on the stereo. Mystic and Wirenut walked toward me, smiling. Wirenut's lips moved, but I didn't hear a word.

The walls narrowed in, and I swallowed the sickness in my mouth. Champagne, even a sip, on an empty stomach with a muscle relaxer. Not a good combination with *FLYING.*

Heat flashed through my body, then icy dampness. I swayed.

"Somesome thingthing's wrongwrong withwith GiGi-GiGi." Parrot's voice echoed through my ears.

Mystic doubled into twin thick-necked clairvoyants. They both grabbed me. I squeezed my eyes shut, and it made the dizziness worse.

"Lay her down on the carpet," TL instructed.

My whole world tilted. I pried my eyelids open. Fuzzy doubles of everyone's faces crowded my space. I tried to push back.

TL and his duplicate put their hands on my shoulder. "Lie still."

I swallowed another wave of nausea.

"She's gonna hurl," both Beakers announced a little too enthusiastically.

The TLs unsnapped my jeans and pulled my T-shirt out. "Give her some breathing room." The blurry doubles took a step back. "Has she eaten today?"

"I saw her sucking on a lollipop earlier." Bruiser and her twin placed a wet rag on my forehead. The coolness made me moan.

The TLs fanned me with a magazine. "Champagne on an empty stomach."

Bruiser put all four hands over her two mouths. "With a prescription muscle relaxer."

The TLs continued to fan me. "What's she taking muscle relaxers for?"

Nooo. I shook my head, and all the fuzzy doubles bounced around.

"Her period."

EIGHTEEN

Closing my eyes, I gingerly reclined my first-class seat. The sedative TL gave me hours ago was long gone. Gone before it had had a chance to kick in. I'd never thrown up so much in my life. Two times at the ranch, once in the limo on the way to the airport, two times in the terminal, and once just now in the plane's bathroom. And we hadn't even taken off yet.

If I hadn't been so nervously sick, I might have enjoyed my first time in a limo. If I didn't need to dry-heave again, I might be embarrassed that TL, Jonathan, *and* David saw me *hurling*, as Beaker so enthusiastically put it yesterday.

And Bruiser had announced to everyone that I got the big P. Oooh. She definitely had it coming when I returned from Ushbania.

If I got back. Bad guys, national security, bombs, a kidnapping. Big-time stuff. Things might not go right. I could really screw up.

Not to worry, Audrey, my modeling instructor, had reassured me when she came by the ranch to see me off. Hives had been her main concern. *Hives.* I was facing the biggest fear of my life, and she was worried about some little red rashy dots.

"Miss January, are you sure I can't get you something?"

Miss January? Oh, yeah, that's me. My modeling name. I forced my eyelids open. The flight attendant looked more nervous than I felt. Probably thought I'd throw up all over her first-class area, and she'd have to clean it up. At least in the fancy seats they call you by your name. Even if it was a fake one.

"Miss January?"

"Ginger ale after we take off," David answered for me.

With a nod, the attendant headed toward the back of the plane.

"How's she doing?" Jonathan whispered from across the aisle.

"She'll make it." David retrieved a blanket from the overhead bin. He tucked it in around me, then sat back down.

Funny how a tucked-in blanket can make a person feel better. Like armor protecting against the bad stuff. The bogeyman in a dark orphanage, shadows in an unknown foster home, or plain emptiness in my first dormitory . . .

Shaking off my momentary walk into the past, I concentrated on the here and now.

Jonathan, David, TL, and I were dressed and acting our roles for the mission. TL gave us fake passports with matching false IDs. We each had memorized our made-up backgrounds. That made twice for me in the past few months. Once when the IPNC recruited me and I became Kelly Spree/GiGi, and again for this mission.

My new modeling name? Jade January. Ridiculous or what? The IPNC actually employed a person who made up false IDs. What a job. Guess there're a lot of secret agents on missions if someone works all day creating their fake backgrounds.

In between worrying over hives and posture, Audrey picked out clothes and packed for me. She dressed me in knee-length, brown suede boots and a thigh-length, crème sweater dress. At the last second, a stylist snipped layers into my shoulder-length blond hair and made me promise not to pull it back in a ponytail. What he didn't know wouldn't kill him.

They'd also worked on David, TL, and Jonathan. David, my personal photographer, wore faded jeans, a white T-shirt, black leather jacket, and boots. He'd grown stubble and carried his camera equipment on the plane. His yum factor hit twenty on a scale of one to ten.

TL, my bodyguard, wore a black suit and matching shades. He hadn't taken the sunglasses off once. Very mysterious, serious demeanor. Other than in the limo, he hadn't spoken or showed any emotion.

Jonathan, my modeling agent, wore a white suit. A purple eye patch replaced his usual black one and matched his purple silk shirt and shoes. His bald head gleamed from where the hair stylist had buffed it. As soon as we stepped from the limo into public view, Jonathan and his cell phone had been inseparable. Part of his modeling-agent role.

"Ladies and gentlemen, this is Captain Steve Brusher speaking. Welcome aboard Air Transport commercial flight ten-eleven. Flying nonstop from San Belden, California, to Prost, Ushbania . . ."

Beneath the blanket, I dug my fingernails into my palms. I could do this. I knew I could. Just because my parents died in a plane crash didn't mean I would die in one.

" . . . It's going to be a beautiful flight today. Clear skies.

Current temperatures in Prost are five above zero. We'll be reaching an altitude of thirty thousand feet . . ."

Thirty thousand feet. Really high up. Over the ocean. Something goes wrong. No place to land. Only the water. I squeezed my eyes shut and concentrated on calming breaths. *In. Then out. In. Then out.* Like TL had taught me.

" . . . flotation device beneath the seat. Should the cabin lose pressure, an oxygen mask will fall from the overhead bin. Reach up and pull the mask taut and put it over your nose and mouth. Oxygen will be flowing even though the bag does not inflate. Please place your own mask on before attending to children . . ."

I caught my breath as the memory flooded back. Six years old. Dangling oxygen masks. My dad had put his over me first. Because of him, I survived the crash. He pushed me free. I swam to the surface knowing he and Mom would be right behind.

Gripping my seat flotation. Dark. Wet. Debris popping up around me. Curling my legs up as tight as I could in the water. Searching . . . searching . . . everyone surfaced but them. *Daaadddyyy! Mooommmyyy!* Why didn't they surface?

"Shhh," David said softly. He smoothed a tissue over my cheeks, and I realized I was crying. He slipped his arm beneath the blanket and covered my clenched fist with his hand.

In. Then out. In. Then out. I paced my breathing, blocking everything else.

The plane slowly moved, backing away from the terminal. David ran his thumb across my fist, back and forth, in a soft caress. I gradually stopped concentrating on my breaths and focused all my energy on his tender touch. His thumb worked its way inside my fist, circling my palm and stroking the underside of my fingers.

I sighed with the release of tension and stress. He linked fingers with me and brought our hands palm to palm.

The engines roared and the plane sped down the runway. I opened my eyes and gazed out the window as the jet lifted off. The buildings and trees got smaller and smaller. Sometime later, clouds filled my view . . . and I smiled. I made it. I actually made it.

"Here's your ginger ale."

I turned my attention to the flight attendant, who placed the glass in the armrest's cup holder.

"Thank you."

David squeezed my hand as she strode off. "Better?

I nodded.

"Good." He slipped a rolled-up magazine from his jacket pocket with his free hand, spread it across his lap, flipped a few pages, then began reading.

Idly I studied the clouds outside my window, and one by one my brain cells zeroed in on our clasped hands. The warm, slightly roughened texture of his. Our linked fingers. His thumb skimming back and forth in a subconscious action. Normal. Like we had held hands hundreds of times before. Amazing how his touch provided the comfort I needed.

Was he thinking about my hand in his? He seemed preoccupied with his magazine. Maybe it was an act. Maybe he was just as focused on our hands as I was.

Then again, probably not. David was eighteen. He'd probably held hands with plenty of girls. He'd probably kissed lots, too. He'd probably even done more than that . . .

With the last thought, my palm immediately went

clammy. I didn't want to stop holding hands, but I didn't want to gross him out, either.

Stupidstupidstupid.

He saw me as a little sister. He'd said so before. He held my hand like a big brother would hold a little sister's. Although his caressing thumb didn't feel very brotherly-sisterly.

Pulling his hand free from mine, he unclipped his seat belt. "Bathroom break." He took a lollipop from his jacket pocket and handed it to me. "It's grape."

How unbelievably sweet. "Thanks."

Jonathan stepped across the aisle and took David's seat. "You're looking better. Let's talk about . . ."

Grudgingly, I focused on his words, but my mind screamed, *YOU'RE IN DAVID'S SEAT, YOU BIG EYE-PATCH GALOOT!*

NINETEEN

Turned out I spent most of the sixteen-hour flight beside everyone *but* David. Jonathan had carried on a brief agent/model conversation with me, more for show than anything. When he got done, TL and David were engaged in a deep conversation. It went on for so long, Jonathan fell asleep. Hours later he woke up, but David had fallen asleep. Hours after that I woke up, didn't realize I'd fallen asleep, and noticed that TL was sitting beside me. Apparently Jonathan had challenged David to a rousing game of tic-tac-toe.

Then a late-night dinner came and a movie, and everyone stayed in their shuffled-around spots. By the time the flight ended, David was back beside me, but so engrossed in his magazine that every chance of holding hands fizzled away.

Now, as we stood outside our hotel suite, I rolled my eyes at my immaturity. We were on a top secret national mission, and my biggest worry was holding hands. Jeez.

Our bellboy swiped a key card through the electronic

lock, and we all filed into the suite. Romanov owned this hotel. All the models were staying at it.

Jonathan gave the young bellboy some money, and he left. TL rubbed his chin, then brushed imaginary lint from his shoulder. Our signal to get into character.

"I swear that boy stank." I flounced over to the blue velvet couch and plopped down. The perfect, spoiled-rotten model. "Haven't they heard of soap in this country?"

TL and David unsnapped the buckles from their belts, leaving two black leather straps dangling in place. Starting at the door, they worked in opposite directions, scanning every lamp, door frame, decoration, piece of furniture, light switch, and whatever else they could find. The tips of the belt buckles glowed steady green. It would blink red if it detected a bug. A brilliant device that Chapling had created years ago.

Jonathan meandered over to the marble bar. "Now, honey, you're just tired from the long trip." He took a crystal glass from a silver tray, some ice from the freezer, and poured in seltzer water. "Little bit of this, a good nap, and you'll be all better."

His light still glowing steady green, David disappeared into one of the bedrooms.

"Yuck." I plunked my high-heeled boots onto the dark wood coffee table. "If you don't have lime, I'm not drinking it. I'd rather have a regular soda."

"Regular soda?" Jonathan gasped, and I almost laughed. "Wash your mouth out. Do you know how many calories that has?"

David came out of a bedroom at the same time as TL stepped from a bathroom, both their buckle tips still glowing green. David strode across the red-carpeted living room toward me, focused intently on his buckle detection device.

"But all I've eaten today is yogurt," I whined. "One little soda won't hurt me." Amazing that people worried about stuff like calories. What a waste of valuable brain time.

"Tsk, tsk." Jonathan shook his finger at me. "Every calorie becomes a cheese dimple on your thigh."

David ran the detection device over, around, and beneath the coffee table where my feet sat propped. He scanned the couch, leaning around me and stepping over me. He squatted and inspected the underside. With every movement his cologne drifted around me, hazing my focus. Then he stopped and glanced up at me with his cheek mere inches from my thigh. He raised his dark brows in question. I furrowed mine in response. He widened his eyes and tightened his lips.

What . . . ?

Oh! Quickly I recalled the last thing Jonathan had said. "Cheese dimple," I replied. "Don't be so gross."

David went back to scanning, and I focused all 191 IQ points on Jonathan. I wouldn't have gotten distracted in the first place if David hadn't been kneeling and crawling around me.

"Let's not forget Mary Libby." Jonathan brought me my glass. "She lost her contract with Lovelace Lingerie for a dimple in her right butt cheek."

I held back a grin. Jonathan came up with the craziest lines. Who would've guessed a big, tough, mean-looking guy would play such a great modeling agent. "Oh, puh-lease. Mary Libby lost the contract because she farted on the runway."

Jonathan coughed to cover his laugh. It pleased me I'd finally caught him off guard with one of my lines.

"All clear." TL fastened his buckle back to his belt. "You two are almost *too* good at that."

Jonathan and I exchanged smiles. Did he like stepping out of his old self as much as I did?

TL grabbed the duffel bag that contained all our equipment for the mission. He'd had an Ushbanian IPNC contact deliver it to the hotel's front desk. "Three bedrooms. David and I will bunk in the one next to the door. Jonathan by the balcony. GiGi in the middle."

The guys each grabbed one of my beige leather suitcases, and I retrieved my matching carry-on. Why anyone needed so much luggage stretched beyond my comprehension. Apparently, models did, though.

Odd how I'd lived my whole life out of one knocked-around, dinged, Goodwill hard case.

They deposited my things in the middle bedroom, and it occurred to me that TL had put me in the center on purpose. Probably so they could protect me if anything happened. Another reality check. Bad guys might break in.

I wandered into my private bathroom with its whirlpool tub, white marble sink, blue tiles, and shiny gold fixtures. It was pretty darn fancy for a restroom.

Oooh, expensive body wash and shampoo. Imported from France.

Snatching them off the counter, I unscrewed the caps, inhaled . . . freesia. My favorite. And a loofah to go with it!

"Hey." David tapped on the open bathroom door. "Want me to help you unpack?"

Quickly, I fumbled everything back, my stomach fluttering with embarrassment. He'd caught me excited over shampoo and a loofah. I could be such a dork. "Urn, that's okay. I can handle it."

"You sure? I didn't think you knew how. You're still living out of that ratty suitcase at the ranch."

Who was he? The suitcase police? "I got it. I'm fine." How hard could it be to hang up some clothes and put stuff in drawers?

He held up his hands. "All right."

The doorbell buzzed, and everyone broke into action. David and I sprinted to the living room. He grabbed his camera from his bag and trucked it over to the balcony windows. I snatched a fashion magazine from the coffee table and plopped down on the couch. Jonathan whipped out his cell phone and slipped onto a wrought-iron bar stool. We were all in our preassigned positions, ready for any possibility.

TL peered through the peephole. He turned back to us and blinked his left eye twice. Our signal that one of Romanov Schalmosky's men stood outside. My heart raced with the knowledge that a real, live bad guy loomed only a few feet away.

TL rubbed his chin, then brushed imaginary lint from his shoulder. *Get into character.* David lifted his camera and began clicking off pictures. I quickly popped gum in my mouth and proceeded to flip through the magazine, as bored and spoiled as ever. Jonathan struck up a fake conversation on his cell phone. TL slipped on his shades and opened the door.

The bad guy stepped into our suite. I tried to seem indifferent to the intrusion, but jeez, the guy was huge. Like an evil-power-lifter kind of huge.

"Mizz Jade January?"

Cool Count Dracula accent. I blew a bubble and snapped it.

"Yeah?"

"Joo are cordially invited to Mizter Schalmosky's home." He cut his gaze to David, Jonathan, TL, then back to me. "Alone."

TWENTY

<%bLkco;/Tpircs+!>
   *<=*ptth *= l!attstli!/ %csorrtetat%>*
   <#n8li# :Ius en/: g<bsu>3<bsu>g>

Ow! I scowled down at TL's hand squeezing my forearm, then over at him. He gave me a barely discernible shake of the head. How had he done that? How'd he know I zoned out?

I glanced at my watch. Exactly thirty-seven minutes and two seconds had passed since we left our hotel room.

The elevator in Romanov's castle dinged, and his goon motioned us to step out. I clicked my brain cells into focus and promised myself I wouldn't let my thoughts veer again. I really did need to work on that. Getting sidetracked was one of my biggest weaknesses. Especially at some of the most inopportune moments, like this one. When I was about to meet the ultimate bad guy, Romanov Schalmosky.

Thank God TL had insisted on coming. Thank God Romanov's goon let him. As my bodyguard, it actually made a lot of sense for TL to escort me. David and Jonathan, however, stayed at the hotel. Having our team split up made me edgy. Maybe that's why my mind had wandered to code. TL had trained me for just this sort of thing, but reality sure differed from simulation. A lot.

We strode down a long tiled-floor hallway lined with gleaming wood walls. I concentrated on holding my head high and shoulders back like the modeling instructor had taught me. At the very end of the hallway stood a door. It slowly opened as we approached.

I fought the urge to scope out the cameras. How else would they have known to open the door? Unless they'd installed potentio detectors in the floor or maybe laser sensors in the walls. *Neat.* My pulse raced with geeky tech excitement. I started to reach for my notepad and pencil at the exact same second I remembered I wasn't GiGi. I was Jade January, model. And models didn't carry notepads and pencils.

Another one of Romanov's goons, as huge as the first one, appeared in the open doorway holding a machine gun. My eyes and mouth popped open in sync. TL stepped in front, shielding me, and I grabbed onto the back of his suit jacket and scooted in close. Exactly what GiGi *or* Jade January would've done.

Goon number one, standing behind us, spoke to Goon number two with the machine gun. Their Ushbanian sounded deep and guttural, like they had a bad cold. Whatever Goon number one said made Goon number two move aside.

"Joo may enter," said Goon number one. "Mizter Schalmosky iz waiting."

TL slid his hand around and dislodged my fingers from his jacket. Reluctantly I released him, but wanted more than anything to stay pressed up securely against him.

As we entered a tiny waiting room, another door automatically opened, and a woman appeared. She was small, business-sophisticated, with Hawaiian features and shiny dark hair slicked back into a low bun.

"Good afternoon, Miss January." The beautiful woman extended her hand, and I shook it. "My name is Nalani Kai. I'm Mr. Schalmosky's personal assistant. Please don't be frightened by the formalities." She indicated Goon number one and Goon number two with a nod.

I couldn't help but smile at her. Her friendly demeanor eased my nerves. "Thank you for inviting me."

She nodded again graciously, and focused beyond my shoulder to where TL stood. Although her expression didn't change, I got the distinct impression she thought my body-guard had it going on. *Hey, he's a hottie,* I wanted to tell her, *go for it.* They seemed about the same age. Why not?

Oh, yeah, she worked for the bad guys. Bummer. Maybe she didn't know they were bad. She seemed too nice to be working for the other side.

Nalani led us down another gleaming wood hallway and around a corner. She motioned us to proceed through an archway into an office as big as our living room back at the ranch. Straight ahead at a desk sat a gray-haired man dressed in a dark suit.

Behind him a bank of windows looked out over an indoor garden. Beyond that, snow drifted against the green-house walls. A stone fireplace to the right warmed the room to the point of too hot.

The gray-haired man peered up from his paperwork as we entered. Yellow tinted his skin. Beside him sat an oxygen tank. A tube ran from it into his nose.

He nodded at Nalani. "Zank you. Zat'll be all." Cool Count Dracula accent, like his goons. "Joo, sir"—he nodded to TL—"may stand against zee back wall."

As TL moved to the rear of the room, I wondered how he liked being given an order when he was always the one in command.

The gray-haired man came around the front of the desk, rolling his oxygen tank with him. It clicked, sending out an audible burst of oxygen.

He stood eye level with me as he extended his hand. "Velcome to my home. I am Romanov Schalmosky." His spooky, pitch-black eyes sent a chill dancing down my spine.

I accepted his hand. *Omigod, I'm shaking hands with THE bad guy.* "Thank you for inviting me, Mr. Schalmosky. I'm Jade January. So nice to meet you."

"Please, call me Romanov."

"Thank you, Romanov. Feel free to call me Jade."

He shook his head. "I vill call you Mizz January."

Okay. "As you wish."

He indicated the two brown leather chairs in front of his desk. I sat in one and he took the other. He held out his hand, and I stared at it a second . . . *oh!*

Ick. I have to hold hands with him?

Trying my best to act flattered that he wanted to hold hands with me, I reached out. He placed my palm on his knee and with a pat, settled his cool, dry hand on top. I fought the urge to glare at TL.

"Mizz January, I like to meet vith all my models before their debut at my school. I enjoy a superior reputation for producing zee best of zee best. You vill maintain zee upmost ladylike demeanor. If any of my associates tell me differently, you vill be returned to zee States without any questions asked. Do vee understand each other?"

I swallowed the enormous nervous lump in my throat. "Yes, sir."

"It iz your place to look pretty and be a lady. If you have a tendency to snoop, correct zee imperfection now. If I catch you somewhere you are not supposed to be, you vill suffer zee consequences."

Consequences? What consequences?

He patted my hand. "Zere. Enough said. You vill be famous. I guarantee it. All my models are."

I didn't want to be famous. I wanted to get the H-E-double-L out of here. This guy scared the crap out of me.

"Get some rest. Take zee day off. Tomorrow night I am hozting a party for all my models. I know your agent and photographer traveled vith you. They are more than velcome to attend." He lifted my hand from his knee and pressed wet lips to the back of it.

Yuk.

"And you, my love, vill be my date."

What?!

TWENTY-ONE

David approached TL and me as we entered our hotel suite. "We downloaded new intel from Chapling," David said as we closed the door. "The statue and microsnipet may be at Romanov's home."

Numbly, I shuffled to my room.

"What's wrong with her?" I heard David ask. "What happened?"

I sank down on my bed, staring at the red carpet. Machine guns. Big, scary goons. A creepy old guy with a not-so-cool Count Dracula accent and spooky, pitch-black eyes. Consequences if I snooped. *And you, my love, vill be my date.*

With a nauseated stomach, I closed my eyes and lay back. What had I been thinking, accepting this mission? I was in way over my head. Calm, cool, and collected were not in my vocabulary. I was scared out of my genius mind. Seriously, TL had to find someone else. He had to. I couldn't do this.

As I rolled over and curled up on the bed, TL's words echoed through my head. From the start, you proved to be adept at your cover. You went about your day-to-day activities smoothly, naturally, and without second thoughts. It's almost as if you've been here for months instead of a few weeks. I'm impressed with how seamlessly you merged into this world.

I wouldn't be sending you if I didn't have complete confidence in your ability. Always remember that.

Whether I wanted it or not, our nation's security depended on this mission. TL had put all his faith in me. David needed my skills to find his dad.

"Hey."

I opened my eyes. David stood alongside the bed, staring down at me.

"TL told me what happened. You're going to be fine, GiGi. None of us will let anything happen to you. I promise. I know seeing all this stuff in real life is scary as hell. Especially for someone like you. I grew up in this world. You've been a part of it for only a couple of months. No one I know has ever been thrown into a mission in such a short time. We all recognize that. But let me tell you something. The IPNC would never have sent you, no matter the time crunch of the mission, if they weren't completely confident you would do it. Okay? You *can* do this. I know you can."

If Mr. Share weren't involved, would David still be saying all this? Immediately I pushed the negative question from my mind. Of course, he would still be saying it. Last thing I needed was to question my own teammates.

"Thanks." I sat up. Okay. I could do this. I could.

David smiled. "You're welcome. We have nothing to do but wait for this party. Romanov has left strict orders that none of the models leave the hotel until tomorrow night."

"Must be nice to order people around like that."

David chuckled. "Yeah, really. If you feel like cards, come on out."

I took a long bath instead and then tried to get some sleep. The next day, I gave myself a manicure and pedicure. I practiced my modeling walk. I practiced putting on makeup. I keyed code. I watched a little TV. I tried to sleep, but didn't. When room service arrived, I ate a little bit. I went back over everything in my mind. I'd never been so wound up in my life. I just wanted everything to be over with.

All three guys tried talking to me. I couldn't focus on a conversation. I managed to sleep some. And finally, *finally,* it was time to get ready for the party.

I dug in my purse for a lollipop and the "cheat sheet." *Here,* Audrey had said, handing me the paper. *This will help you know what to wear when.*

I had never used a cheat sheet before in my life. How ridiculous was it that I needed one for clothing?

After slipping the banana lollipop in my mouth, I scanned the typed paper. Two columns. The left column listed all the possible functions, situations, or outings I would encounter as a model. The right column detailed which outfit and accessories I should wear.

Party at Romanov's home I found on the left, looked across to the right . . . *One-piece silver jumpsuit.*

I groaned. I *hated* the silver jumpsuit. It was so hard to get on and off.

Forty-five minutes later I emerged from my room in the skin tight one-piece, complete with silver stilettos and dangling diamond earrings. Too bad the front of the jumpsuit V-necked down between my boobs. It was like zero degrees outside. What I really needed to be wearing was a turtleneck and a pair of flannel-lined pants.

"I'm ready."

TL, Jonathan, and David all glanced up from the living room, where they sat discussing a map. No one uttered a word. They just stared at me.

Automatically, my brain clicked through a checklist, making sure I hadn't forgotten something.

Hair not in ponytail. *Check.*

Makeup. *Check.*

Earrings. *Check.*

Underwear. *Check.*

Jumpsuit zipped. *Che—*

Jonathan let out a low, slow whistle. "Zowee, girl. If I were twenty years younger, you'd have to beat me off with a stick."

"Oh." My face heated with his compliment. I immediately looked at David, but he diverted his gaze.

TL rose from the couch. "I need to throw on a tie. Give her the devices."

He headed to his room and disappeared inside.

Jonathan followed. "TL, one last thing . . ." he was saying as he left David and me alone.

David grabbed two black boxes from the end table, one square and one rectangular, and crossed the room to me. "You'll wear two pieces of equipment tonight. A tracking device and the microsnipet detector."

David flipped the top on the square box. Inside lay a tiny brown flake. He pressed his index finger to it. "It's a freckle. As long as this stays on your body, I'll—I mean, we'll know where you are."

He took a step closer, and his cologne zinged my synapses. In my stilettos, we stood eye to eye. He searched my face, neck, and chest. "So . . . so where do you want it?"

Was it possible I affected him more than he let on? My heart danced a happy pitter-patter.

"It should be on your neck or chest. Unlike cotton fabrics, some, like this with metallic threads, tend to interrupt the signal, and you were in a cotton turtleneck yesterday. Romanov has seen your face. He'll know if there's something different. So neck or chest?"

I didn't answer. I couldn't. His nearness made me mute. I shook my head.

"Saliva adheres it." He touched his tongue to it and then pressed the brown flake to my collarbone. As he held it there, his dark gaze traveled slowly up my neck and face and locked onto my eyes. We stared at each other with only inches of space between us. I became hyperaware of his moist finger, his breath skittering across my cheek, and my heart pounding so hard it reached my ears.

"Ready." TL emerged from his room, followed by Jonathan. "Got the finger pads?"

"Uh . . ." David took a quick step back, and I grabbed onto a bar stool to steady myself. "Yeah. Right here."

He opened the rectangular box. Side by side lay the four transparent pads that I had assisted Chapling in developing. One for each of us, specially designed for our middle fingers. Thin, silicone-based, invisible once in place. Activated by magnetics. They were programmed to send a quick, hot jolt if one of us touched the statue containing the microsnipet.

David passed the box around. I pressed my middle finger to the remaining pad, and it suctioned on like it had a life of its own.

TL checked his watch. "Let's go."

Our black limo drove through town out into the country. For miles around nothing existed but fields and woods, everything white from a fresh winter snow. We pulled up to Romanov's castle exactly twenty-seven minutes and thirteen seconds later. I knew this because timekeeping was part of David's job, and he'd just told us.

We cleared the guards and entered the iron gates. Where it had been empty yesterday, shiny cars now lined the cobblestone driveway. Even in the nighttime, the vibrant colors stood out. Red Rolls-Royce. White Ferrari. Yellow Porsche. Orange Mercedes. And the variety went on and on.

Pretty impressive, if I said so myself.

Tiny, white lights twinkled in the trees and shrubs lining Romanov's castle and property. Like a fairy tale, only my prince was a creepy, old guy.

One big goon opened our limo's door, and we all piled out. I squinted against the icy-cold air and pulled my white, faux fur coat around me. The goon escorted us up the castle's front steps. Not the same entrance TL and I had used yesterday. We'd entered through the side.

Two large wooden doors I estimated at twenty feet tall opened, gushing out warmth, light, and music. We stepped in and the doors closed behind us. Standing on a marble landing, we gazed down at the festivities in the enormous ballroom. Gorgeous women, hot guys, and old men. Dressed in gowns, tuxedos, suits, and even jeans. Drinking, dancing, and talking.

We were right on time, but the number of partygoers already here implied our tardiness. Guess people didn't mess with fashionably late when Romanov was involved.

"Mizz January. Velcome."

I didn't have to look to know who that voice belonged to. Inwardly I groaned, but outwardly I plastered on a smile and turned. "Romanov!"

He held his hands out and I took them. He wasn't wearing his oxygen tube, but his yellow skin looked even more jaundiced under these lights.

With wet lips, he kissed both my cheeks in greeting and then introduced himself to David and Jonathan.

Romanov turned me around and slipped my coat off, skimming his chilly fingers down my arms as he went. I fought the urge to gag. "You are very enticing this evening." He held his arm out. "Shall vee?"

I chanced a quick glance at David. He quickly snapped his attention to the party. With a slap on the back to TL and a quick nod to Jonathan, he made his way down the steps. I shouldn't have peeked at him. I could blow my cover doing something so stupid.

Romanov silently indicated a spot against the back wall where other bodyguards were standing. TL nodded and headed off in that direction. Jonathan trailed behind him. I experienced a flash of panic at being left alone, but immediately squashed it down. My teammates knew exactly where I was.

Sliding my hand into the crook of Romanov's arm, I followed him down the marble stairs and along the perimeter of the ballroom. More than one set of eyes turned curiously in our direction.

Smile. Suck in stomach. Shoulders back. Smile. Suck in stomach. Shoulders back.

I chanted Audrey's commands so my brain wouldn't focus on my flip-flopping stomach. Being escorted by Romanov was a privilege. I met the other models' jealous stares with a Jade January, he-likes-me-better-than-you preen, when all I really wanted to do was hand him over with a *here, take him.*

We stopped at one of the many bars positioned around the room. "What would you like?"

"Seltzer with a twist of lime, please."

"Good girl. Alcohol haz too many calories."

Good girl? What was I, his pet?

A young, bald guy approached from the right. He gave me a cursory glance as he spoke to Romanov in Ushbanian. At least I assumed it was Ushbanian. The bartender set my glass down, and I took a tiny sip.

Romanov lifted my hand and placed a damp kiss on my knuckles. "Pleaze excuse me. I'll only be a few minutes."

He and the bald guy rounded the bar and disappeared through a door. Hmm, wonder where they're going? To do some bad-guy thing for sure. I'd seen enough movies: bad-guy leader excuses himself from joyful get-together. Shows up in basement where other bad guys are waiting. Good guy is chained to chair, bloody and beaten. Won't give bad guys information. Bad-guy leader orders torture until good guy gives in.

I focused on the pink marble floor beneath my stilettos. If only I possessed laser vision and could see the basement and tell whether or not a good guy was chained there.

A pair of shiny black shoes stepped into my line of sight. I looked up at a gorgeous guy. Blond. Green eyes. Impeccably dressed in a light gray suit. He bowed. "Mizter Schalmosky asked me to dance with you. He vill be longer than expected."

I nodded, said thank you, and slipped my arm through his. "I'm Jade January. What's your name?"

"Mizz January, you may call me Petrov."

"Petrov." I tried his name, staring at his scrumptious face. Too bad he was a bad guy.

We made our way onto the packed dance floor and

through the gyrating bodies. He stopped somewhere in the middle and began dancing. Quickly, I recalled my lessons from last week and moved my shoulders and feet to the beat. I scanned the ballroom for my teammates (being tall has its advantages), turned a slow-hipped circle, and stopped.

There danced David with one, two, three, *four* beautiful, perfect, exotic, seductive, gorgeous models. They sandwiched him, two in front, two in back, doing a grind move straight off a music video. He lifted his arms, laughing, getting quite the groove on.

He winked at me. I snapped out of my momentary trance and kept right on dancing. *Okay, David's role is to be a flirtatious, single photographer,* logic reminded me. But he acted the role a little *too* well, if you asked me.

"You should see the statue in the ladies' room," I heard a woman yell over the music.

Statue. I signaled Petrov, and he leaned in. "I need to go to the restroom. I'll be back."

He shook his head. "I vill valk vith you."

Pouting flirtatiously, I touched his arm. "I'd like privacy, please. I'll meet you at the bar in ten minutes." I pivoted and strode off, not giving him a chance to argue.

Please don't follow me. Pleasepleaseplease don't follow me.

Passing David and his models, I scratched the back of my head with my left hand. Our statue signal.

I did the same as I crossed in front of TL, who stood with the other bodyguards along the back wall. Like soldiers, lined up, a few feet of space between them. All without expressions.

Jonathan sat on a stool at one of the bars. He sipped an

umbrella drink while carrying on a loud conversation with another beautiful model.

Statue-signaling him, I meandered past the bar. Good. All my teammates knew now. I pushed open the bathroom door and found myself bringing up the rear of a long line. Figured.

Taking my place, I surreptitiously peered around the lounge area that preceded the sinks. Straight-backed couches, fancy wood end tables, delicate wrought-iron stools, makeup mirrors, but no statue.

One woman came out, and another went in. The line inched forward.

A wall divided the lounge area from the sinks. From where I stood, a mirror gave me a clear shot. No statue in there, either.

Maybe this wasn't the only bathroom. A big place like this had to offer more than one, especially with all the females. "Excuse me."

The short, elderly lady beside me arched a penciled-in eyebrow as a response.

"Is this the only bathroom?"

"No. Zere is one across zee ballroom."

"Thanks." Probably the one with the statue.

One woman came out, and another went in. The line inched forward. A couple more models came in and took their place behind me.

Jeez, how many toilets were there? One? Never understood why it took girls so long in the bathroom. You got in, did your business, and got out. What's the big deal?

Clearly, this had to be the wrong bathroom. Okay, I'd make some spoiled, rich model comment about the wait and hoof it across the ballroom.

A tall redhead passed me on the way out. "I have to take a picture of that statue."

Statue? I perked up.

"I know," her tall blond friend agreed. "It's the funniest thing. Wonder who made it?"

One woman came out, and another went in. The line inched forward.

Just the short old lady now and then I could get in. The statue must be in the toilet area. I tapped my stiletto and peeked at my silver watch. Eighteen minutes. Petrov expected me in ten. Ugh.

One woman came out, and the old lady went in. I inched forward, glanced across the sink room to the toilets. Sure enough, one door. What had Romanov been thinking? You can't have one toilet in a ballroom bathroom.

The old lady came out. "Toilet's clogged."

The models behind me sighed and strode from the bathroom.

I crossed the tile floor, went in, and closed the door. I stood, taking in all the art decorating the huge room. Portraits and landscapes hung from the pink walls. Figurines stood on dozens of small wood shelves. In the corner sat the clogged toilet and beside it the statue.

It stood at least six feet tall and depicted a naked Romanov surrounded by four of his models, each wearing a robe. Luckily, one of the models' legs covered his privates. Funny, I would have expected the opposite. Romanov in the robe and the models naked.

Quickly, I put my middle finger on the statue. No heat. Both relief and disappointment hit me. Relief that I'd have more time to prepare for the microsnipet extraction. Disappointment that I'd have to go through all this again.

I opened the door, raced across the tile, rounded the wall into the lounge area, and ran smack into David.

"What are you doing?" I hissed.

"You've been in here forever," he hissed back. "We got worried."

"Petrov, what is it?" I heard a woman ask from outside the bathroom.

David and I both froze.

"Mizz January has been in zere far too long. Mizter Schalmosky iz waiting for her."

"Well, I heard the bathroom's out of order, but I'll check and see." The door creaked open.

Before I could panic, David quickly spun me around and yanked down my jumpsuit zipper.

TWENTY-TWO

Nalani pushed into the bathroom and came to an abrupt stop. Her eyes widened as the door swung shut behind her. "Oh." She let out a nervous laugh. "I didn't realize . . ."

"Looks like what this isn't." I shook my head. "I mean, this isn't what it looks like."

"Of course, this isn't what it looks like." David maintained a solid grip on the unzipped, very open back of my jumpsuit, prohibiting me from stepping away. "Stupid thing," he mumbled, and I realized he was pretending my zipper was stuck.

"As you can see"—I elaborated on his ruse, avoiding eye contact with Nalani—"the clogged toilet ran everybody off. I, um, accidentally dropped something down my jumpsuit. And then I, uh, came in here to get it out, and now I can't seem to get this darn—"

David's fingers and warm breath brushed my lower back. My brain went blank. I stood there, aware I should be saying something, but for the life of me couldn't recall what. He gave my fastener a firm tug, and I snapped back to the moment.

"I can't get this darn zipper up. I stuck my head out the door, and he"—I jabbed my thumb over my shoulder—"was the only person within yelling distance." I sighed, all bothered and impatient.

"There." David dragged the zipper up the length of my spine, under my hair to my neck, leaving a shiver prickling my skin. He turned to Nalani. "You're Mr. Schalmosky's assistant, right?"

She inclined her head. "Yes."

"I heard there's a garden of statues. I'd like to take pictures of Jade out there. It'll round out her portfolio."

"Certainly. I'll escort you and then let Mr. Schalmosky know where you'll be." Nalani peeked at her slim diamond watch and motioned for us to follow.

With legs I hoped appeared steadier than they felt, I crossed to the door and followed her out. We'd almost gotten busted. If not for David's quick thinking, there was no telling what might have happened. Clearly, I was not cut out to go on missions. I did much better behind closed doors, safely sitting at a computer. Lots of time to think and formulate plans.

But coming up with a story like his stuck-zipper idea had been pretty darn ingenious. Gave me a little excited rev once I got focused. Once I ignored the fact that he'd seen my entire bare, braless back.

Fifteen minutes later, I leaned against the black iron rail as David snapped pictures.

Clickclick. Clickclick.

Behind me spread a conservatory with statues nestled among the greenery. Above, the transparent ceiling of the greenhouse showed the night sky, stars, and snow floating down. To my right, French doors led back into the ballroom. Petrov stood there, watching us. Obviously, Romanov didn't trust David and me out here alone. Smart man. Bad guys didn't become bad guys by trusting people.

"Good." *Clickclick. Clickclick.* "Now arch your back."

Arch my back? I wanted to narrow my eyes at David, but refrained. After all, Petrov loomed nearby. I arched my back, or in other words stuck out my boobs, and smiled for the camera.

"No smile. I need pout. Sexy. Full lips." *Clickclick. Clickclick.*

Pout? Sexy? Okay, David was taking it too far.

"Pout for me, baby." Clickclick. Clickclick.

Baby?

"Perfect!" *Clickclick. Clickclick.* "Break." David slipped the camera strap over his head and crossed the brick patio to where I stood.

He rearranged a few pieces of my hair while I quietly inhaled his cologne. "You've got to relax," he mumbled. "You don't seem like you know what you're doing. Petrov's going to pick up on your inexperience if you don't focus. Think Jade January, the sexy, spoiled model. Not GiGi, the gorgeous, shy genius."

Gorgeous? My stomach flip-flopped.

David brushed an imaginary something from my shoulder. "Remember, I'm focusing on the statues behind you. I've taken six of the eleven. Move to the left so I can get the remaining five."

With his index finger, he smoothed my eyebrows up, keeping his gaze level with mine. "Think Jade January, not GiGi." He winked, then turned and strolled back to his spot, his backside looking as yummy as ever.

Clickclick. Clickclick.

David waved me to the left, and I moved. He only said the gorgeous thing to keep my mind occupied.

"Right hand on rail. Arch. Left hand in hair." *Clickclick. Clickclick.*

I maneuvered my body into place. And the fiddling with my hair, brushing shoulder, smoothing eyebrows. All meant to keep me sidetracked.

"Chin up. Moisten lips." *Clickclick. Clickclick.*

Chin. Moisten. And the meaningful gaze-deeply-into-my-eyes. Again, meant to keep my thoughts from veering. Oh, he was good. He was real good. Manipulating my brain . . . *and my body, too,* I slowly realized. Standing here all arched with my hand in my hair and moistened lips.

Clickclick. Clickclick.

Time to reverse things. Show *him* a little manipulation game. Played my way.

I spread my legs in a power, Wonder Woman stance. The silver stilettos made me tower over six feet tall. Leveling sultry eyes on the camera, I stared straight into the lens. Straight into his dark brown eyes.

I ran my tongue slowly from one corner of my top lip to the other. Closing my eyes, I tilted my head and arched my back. I skimmed both hands up the front of my skintight jumpsuit, over my cheeks, and into my hair.

Then all my senses returned in a pop, and my heart skipped a beat as my eyes snapped open. No *clickclick, clickclick.* Only silence.

I looked at Petrov first, who stared, eyes wide, mouth hanging open. He obviously didn't think I was an amateur model now. And then to David, standing frozen, camera poised in the air.

"Uh . . ." He fumbled with the protective lens cap. "Th-that's a wrap."

Inwardly, I smiled. Clearly, I'd won the manipulation game. I refrained from doing a victory dance, clapping my hands, chanting, *I won! I won!* I set him off balance more than he set me.

Girl power, schmirl power. I possessed full-blown woman power.

David closed the distance between us, stopping at my side, putting his back to Petrov. "You . . . wow. Not bad."

Curving my lips sensually—at least I hoped it appeared sensual—I arched a brow. "Get all the pictures you needed?" I could not *believe* myself, all confident and self-assured. And enjoying it.

David studied me for long seconds. He shook his head with a chuckle. "Yeah, I got the pics. Now we need to figure out how to touch the statues."

We stared at each other, puzzling, and then it hit me. "Petrov, my night wouldn't be complete without a stroll in the garden. Will you escort me, please?"

"Certainly Mizz January."

I gave David a little pinch on his bristly cheek, which by the spark in his eyes, infuriated him. After I'd accepted Petrov's arm, he unlatched the wrought-iron gate, and we stepped onto a cobblestone walkway.

"I vill do the honors, Petrov." Romanov emerged from the shadows.

Immediately I smiled to cover my frantic thoughts. Oh, dear God, how long had he been standing there? I should've known. TL had trained me better than that. David should've known. He'd been in this business longer than me. Maybe he'd known and it was all part of the act.

I glanced his way. He tapped his collarbone in the same location as my tracking freckle. *I'll—I mean, we'll know where you are.* Breathing easier with the silent reminder, I followed Romanov into the garden as David and Petrov disappeared into the ballroom.

Had Romanov heard David's and my mumblings from his hidden spot? No, not possible, too far away. He'd seen the photography session, though. How could he have missed it? Maybe he missed it. Please, God, make him have missed it.

"I saw your session just now."

Inwardly, I groaned. "I got off to a rough start. Couldn't get my mind focused." Didn't want him to question my modeling ability.

"Yes. But you ended, how do you Americans say, vith a bang?"

"Yes, yes, I ended with a bang." Great, he'd seen me in my woman-power sexy mode. Just what I needed. To get an old man excited.

Okay. Strategy: keep him talking while strolling the garden and touching every statue.

Problem: I wore the microsnipet detector on my right middle finger, which was currently linked with Romanov's jacketed left arm.

"Oh, I must smell that flower." I stepped in front of him and buried my nose in some red plant, which, by the way, smelled like nothing. I then linked my left arm through his right, and we continued down the path.

Romanov gave a detailed explanation of the plant's origin, root system, drainage, blah blah blah. I made little "oh" and "Is that right?" sounds mixed in with occasional nods. All while watching him through wide, I'm-so-interested eyes.

Men, I just began to realize, were so easy to manipulate.

The first of eleven granite statues stood off to the right, approximately three feet tall. A little shepherd boy with a lamb. Surrounded by pink and yellow flowers. Why girls always wanted to smell flowers, I didn't know. They all smelled the same to me. But hey, it had worked to get me close to the statues, so I said, "What beautiful colors. Oh, Romanov, tell me about these."

Slipping from his side, I wandered over and stuck my nose in those, too. Kind of a fruity scent. I pretended to balance myself with my right hand on the lamb's head while sniffing the flowers.

No hot zing in my middle finger. Dang. One down, ten to go.

We continued down the path to the next statue. A teenage guy holding a bow and arrow. This one roughly five feet tall. I ran my fingers over it. No hot zing. "Is this marble?"

Romanov launched into another blah-blah explanation. Imported stones and aging techniques, to which I did the wide-eyed, interested thing.

Third statue stood among purple flowers. Six feet tall. Man holding a book. Bent, sniffed, touched. No hot zing.

"Zis one vill complement your complexion." He snapped off a flower and tucked it behind my ear, trailing his cool finger over my cheek. "You are very beautiful."

Swallowing, I glanced around, unable to see the French doors or the ballroom lights. We'd lost ourselves in the conservatory. Romanov stepped closer. "Do I make you nervous?"

"Yes," I responded before I stopped to think. So much for woman power.

"Good." He chuckled, humorlessly, slow and deep.

Ug. I didn't know how much more of him I could take.

"Shall vee?" He held out his arm, and I carefully took it.

Reality check. Me? Not in charge. He owned complete control of this situation. Stiffly, I matched his casual, confident stride. I needed to get my mind off my sudden nervousness and onto something else. *Relax, GiGi, relax.*

I spied his watch nearly covered by long, black arm hair. Yuck. Never seen one like it before, though. "What kind of watch is that?" I was honestly interested.

"Cuztoom-made. It keeps time."

Yeah, no kidding, Einstein. "What are those other dials and spindles on the inside?"

"Ah, yes. It's complicated for all but zee sharpest of minds."

I resisted the urge to roll my eyes. I could handle it, buddy, believe me. "Will you tell me anyway, please?"

"Why zee interest?"

"I'm shopping for a present. A friend of mine collects watches." Good, quick lie. Not bad.

"Not only are you lovely, but generous, too."

Whatever. But I smiled sweetly anyway. Just tell me the frigging mechanics. Chapling would devour this.

We stopped walking, and he pointed to the spindles. "Zee four inner circles display time in countries of your choice. Press zis button"—he pushed a dial on the side—"and zee four circles switch to other countries."

Hmm. Easy enough to do. Little lead probe soldered to a frequency duct, satellite-controlled.

"Iz good for people who travel."

"What about the infrared glow?"

"How do you know zee term *infrared*?"

Crap. "Video games." I leaned in. "My secret obsession."

"Ah, zee infrared glow is a weapon."

My jaw dropped.

"Vatch." He pointed the watch at a plant, pushed a button, and a red laser shot out, frying the tip of a leaf.

"Cool. A mini infrared beam signaled by a tilt scope." Oh, I wished Chapling were here. I reached for my notepad and pencil, then immediately realized the *huge* mistake I'd made.

Romanov tapped the center of my forehead with his index finger. "I zink you are more intelligent zan you let on."

Oh, crud. I shrugged innocently and decided on honesty. This man would see through anything else. "You're right. I am smart. But models aren't supposed to be. They get further if they pretend to be a little dumb."

"Who told you that?"

"My mother." People tended to pity someone who'd been berated by a parent. And right then I could have used a little pity from Romanov so he would forget about my smarts.

He nodded. "Ah."

I turned away and noticed a statue behind us. Small. One foot tall. Of a puppy Doberman. "Do you have a Doberman?" I asked, walking toward it. "Is that why you had one sculpted?"

"I own ten Dobermans. All trained to attack on command."

Attack on command? My stiletto caught on a cobblestone, and I tripped forward, smashing face-first into the statue. "Ow!"

Romanov rushed toward me. "Mizz January!"

Tasting coppery blood in my mouth, I reached up, grabbing ahold of the Doberman, and a hot zing shot up my arm.

The microsnipet!

TWENTY-THREE

Apparently Romanov's doctor only treated Romanov. So here I sat in our hotel suite roughly thirty minutes later. David applied stinging antiseptic to the corner of my mouth while I held a small bag of ice to my eye. TL sat on the bar stool beside me, studying his iPad. It held digital blueprints of Romanov's home, modeling school, and whatever other buildings we downloaded from the satellite.

With a quiet sigh, I closed my good eye. I knew I would screw up. I just knew it. If it weren't for my klutziness, we'd still be at Romanov's party. I might have been able to tap into the microsnipet and extract the information. We could be rescuing David's dad right now instead of sitting in our suite tending to my stupid cut lip and bruised face.

David shifted, and I opened my eye. He threw the cotton ball away and searched through the first-aid kit. He hadn't uttered a single word to me. No one had. Not in the limo on the way here, nor in the ten minutes we'd been back.

Well, that wasn't exactly true. TL had said *here* right after fixing me a bag of ice in the limo. David had said *sit,* pointing to a bar stool, when we got back to the suite. *Here* and *sit*. Two one-syllable words. Not the silent treatment, but it might as well be.

I tried not to take the quiet personally. They needed time to think, reformulate plans.

Mistakes happen. No one's perfect.

That's what I kept telling myself, but I wanted to be perfect. I didn't want to mess up. I wanted to be a genius in this area of my life, too. Perfect, gifted GiGi saved the day. I wanted TL and everyone to be proud of me. Awed by my talent. I wanted to shine, to be the star. Just once I wanted to be someone I wasn't. And succeed at it.

David peeled the backing off a butterfly bandage, then smoothed it over my lip. My bottom lip quivered, and I immediately stilled it. I would not cry. I absolutely would not cry.

He took the ice bag, set it on the bar behind me, and leaning close, tried to study my eye. I focused on my lap. I would not cry. I absolutely would not cry.

David put his finger under my chin, gently pushing up until our gazes met. His eyes crinkled, and he presented me with a lollipop.

My bottom lip trembled, and I inhaled a choppy breath.

"I'm sorry," I mumbled, a couple of tears streaming down my cheeks.

Playfully, David poked me in the shoulder. "Are you kidding? Everyone screws up. Even our fearless leader. Tell her, TL."

His joking poke caught me off guard. I'd expected a hug. Pat on the back at least.

TL glanced up from his digital maps, saw my blubbery face, but didn't react to it. "Oh, yeah. On my second mission, I knocked out the vice president of the Jalys

Island Nation. Thought he was the head of the opposing force."

"Really?" I sniffed.

He smiled. "Turned out the VP and the head of the bad guys were twins."

I smiled, too, and it dried my tears. Amazing how humor turned a situation around. I'd be having a full-blown, snot-nosed, crying jag right now if they had tried to console me. But then, they probably knew that.

Six quick knocks sounded on the door. Our code that one of us was with one of them.

Snatching the ice bag from the counter, I sprinted across the room and lay down on the couch.

David grabbed the remote, plopped in the chair beside me, and began flipping channels. Quickly, he leaned over, slipped the lollipop into my mouth—hmm, sour apple—and resumed his position.

TL hid the digital maps beneath the bar and went to the door.

"Hey." Jonathan patted TL's cheek. "Forgot my key. Look who I brought."

Nalani stepped inside. "Good evening. I apologize for the late hour." She acknowledged each person, her stare lingering briefly on TL. "I wanted to hand-deliver some-thing to Jade."

Closing the door, TL went back to his bodyguard stance, his face hard and blank. If we hadn't been on a mission and were back living our normal lives, would TL have responded to Nalani's interest? Hmm, or had the love of his life dumped him, emotionally scarring him for all others?

Inside, I grinned. What a little soap-opera writer I'd become.

"How are you?" Nalani crossed to the couch.

I lifted the ice bag from my eye and pulled the lollipop from my mouth. "Never better."

Smiling at my sarcasm, she sat down next to my hips. "I brought a few things." She dug in her purse and pulled out a small white jar. "For your black eye. Apply only at night. It'll be gone in three days. It's a mixture of ary root and dent stem."

How sweet. "Thanks."

"Unfortunately, I don't have anything for your lip. But"—again, she reached inside her purse, this time bringing out a small black velvet box—"I brought a gift from Romanov."

"Oh." Didn't expect that. I opened the lid. Diamond earrings sparkled back at me. "Ohhh, they're beautiful." No one had ever given me jewelry before.

She took my hand. "I'm sorry, but I have to deliver bad news."

Bad news? What bad news?

"I'm sure you understand your injuries prohibit your making your debut from Romanov's school. But he's willing to offer you an invitation to have your debut six months from now."

"Oh, well . . ." How was I supposed to respond? Good thing I already located the microsnipet. Otherwise we'd really be screwed.

"Not to worry, honey." Jonathan strolled over. "You've already got a contract with Lasjet Sportswear."

Nalani kissed my cheek. "You'll enjoy the greatest of success. I'll see you in six months." She made her way to the door, turned with a wave. "Safe journey back to the States."

TL closed the door behind her. He rubbed his nose,

then brushed his shoulder. *Stay in character.* He unclipped his belt-buckle bug detector.

"I like her. She's really sweet. And I like Romanov even more. Check out these rocks."

TL examined the earrings from Romanov. His belt buckle glowed a steady, bug-free green.

"Mmm . . ." Jonathan pursed his lips. "My expert eye says they're only half carats. You should've kissed him. You would've gotten full carats then."

"Gross!"

"All clear." TL clipped his belt buckle back into place. "Get a good night's sleep. We'll infiltrate Romanov's castle tomorrow evening." He strode off to his bedroom.

Get a good night's sleep? Was he kidding? He had to be kidding. Jet lag or not, there was no *way* I'd get a good night's sleep until we were safely back at the ranch.

TWENTY-FOUR

After staring at my bedroom ceiling for an hour, I wandered into the kitchen, found a soda, and settled on the couch with the laptop.

For an hour I worked on my keystroke memorization program and then connected the foldable satellite dish and scrambler. I instant messaged Chapling. Sure enough, he answered.

"Hey."

I jumped, and the computer bounced off my lap onto the cushion beside me.

"Sorry," David whispered.

Heart pounding at the scare, and stomach fluttering because of him, I put the computer back on my lap. I peered across the living room. Blurrily, he lounged against the kitchen counter, his arms and ankles casually crossed. I shoved my glasses on top of my head. "That's okay. How long standing there you been?" I shook my head. "I mean, how long have you been standing there?"

He held his smile for a couple of long seconds, studying me. "Not long."

"Oh, um . . . oh." He'd been watching me? Please, God, promise me I didn't look stupid.

"Can't sleep?"

Shaking my head, I finger-combed my hair, suddenly conscious of the way I looked: huge sweatshirt, baggy pajama bottoms, white athletic socks, black glasses, and a greasy eye from the ointment Nalani had given me.

Dressed the same as me, minus the greasy eye and big glasses, David's yum factor was off the scale. Covering the short distance between us, he sat down on the couch cushion beside me. Off the coffee table, he picked up my proto laser tracker, which I'd brought with me. I'd been working on it for a physics professor back in Iowa. Back in my old life. Seemed like eons ago now. David turned it over. "What exactly *is* this?"

"Something I've been working on."

"What does it do?"

I tried to ignore his knee brushing mine, but failed miserably. "Tracks objects."

"Hmm." David rotated it, studying it. "Looks like a digital camera."

Inside, I did a happy dance. It's exactly what I'd been going for.

"How does it work?"

"Well, uh . . ." This was the part where people tuned me out. My explanations were always too scientific. "A proto neuro chip, when embedded, emits a KED code that disintegrates to CONUSE capable of traveling light speed parallel to its plane of origin based on x, y coordinates—"

"Stop." He held his hand up with a laugh. "Think first, then speak. Make it simple. I'm bright, but not that bright. Start again." No one ever asked me to explain stuff again.

Usually they got a glassed-over look, nodded politely, and went on their way.

I focused on the proto tracker in his hands, really wanting to do this right. "Point the tracker at an object and click the button. A laser beam sends out a microscopic tracking device that embeds itself in the object. Use the LCD screen to follow the object." I switched my gaze from the tracker to his eyes. "How was that?"

David nodded once. "Very nicely done."

My face heated with his compliment.

"Is there anything like this on the market right now?"

"Don't think so."

He tapped the object to my forehead. "Impressive."

"Thanks."

"What about your computer? What's all that code you were typing in?"

"Oh." I shrugged. "Just a program."

"A program that does . . ." He motioned with his hands, encouraging me to elaborate.

It felt so . . . *good* when someone showed genuine interest in me. I took a moment to simplify the explanation in my brain. "It's a program that memorizes keystrokes and mouse clicks. Kinda like those cars that remember the seating and steering position of the driver. This program remembers usage, so if your PC crashes, a separate computer chip holds everything for easy retrieval."

"Sort of like a constant backup of your hard drive but without specifically backing anything up?"

"Right."

"Cool. Does it go with the proto laser tracker?"

"No. They're separate projects." I nodded to the laptop. "I've got Chapling on the line right now."

"Yeah?" David scooted closer, leaning over to type a message. I stared at the side of his face, lit by the glowing blue of the laptop. He laughed and typed something else. I inhaled deeply his soapy David scent mixed with lingering cologne and nearly passed out from his deliciousness.

He glanced over at me, smiling, and his grin slowly faded as he took in every detail of my face.

I didn't breathe.

David focused on my bruised eye. "Hurt?"

I shook my head.

He dropped to my mouth. "How 'bout there?"

Shook my head again. Still not breathing.

"Beautiful," he mumbled.

The laptop dinged, and we both jumped. David slid over a cushion, and I focused on the screen, heart racing, everything a blur.

"What does he say?"

Blinking a few times, I cleared the fog from my brain and concentrated on the words Chapling had typed. "He downloaded intel. Romanov will be gone from his house at eight tomorrow night. He takes half his guards with him when he travels. Chapling advises we wait until then to make our move."

"Good." David pushed up from the couch. "We'll tell TL and Jonathan in the morning." He studied me for a second, like he wanted to say something.

Holding my breath, I waited for his words. Seconds ticked by. He closed his eyes and shook his head, blowing out a breath. "G'night." He made his way across the dimly lit living room, through the kitchen, and into his and TL's room.

I sat on the couch frozen, my mind racing. What was all

that? A you're-so-beautiful-I-don't-know-what-to-do-with-you shake of the head? Or a you're-only-sixteen-I'm-eighteen-are-you-an-idiot blowing out of the breath? But then, why had he called me beautiful?

I dropped my head back with a groan. Life had gone a lot easier when only computers rocked my world.

TWENTY-FIVE

The following evening, I found myself with TL, crouching in the icy dark woods surrounding Romanov's home, watching the castle.

Minutes later, David and Jonathan came up beside us. They'd secured the perimeter, to use TL's lingo, by scouting the property, assuring themselves that none of Romanov's goons lurked about.

TL two-finger-waved David toward the gate. With a nod, David silently slipped from the woods, crossed the road, and came up beneath the guards' building. David's black clothes and face paint, same as we all wore, merged him with the shadows. So much so I had a hard time keeping him in sight.

Inside the small, brick structure, the guard picked up the phone. Right on time.

Beside me Jonathan spoke into his satellite phone, pretending to be Vitro, Romanov's commander, alerting the guard of a disturbance along the east wing. With half the security gone, procedure dictated that the gate goon respond to emergencies.

The guard hung up the phone and, after slipping on his coat, pushed a few buttons on the security panel. He opened the door, rounded the corner, and David jabbed him with a numbing dart. It happened lightning quick. All I caught was David dragging him behind the surrounding bushes.

The guard would be out for about an hour. Jonathan would impersonate him, reporting in every fifteen minutes. All in all, plenty of time to extract the information and get out before anyone even discovered we'd broken in.

David entered the building. Although I couldn't really see him, I knew what he was doing. We'd gone over it right before leaving the hotel suite.

He popped open the security panel, cut a wire, and patched it over. Fusing the video feed. All monitors throughout the castle would display a normal scene. No one, hopefully, would know we were here.

He spliced three wires together, disengaging the electric wrought-iron fence circling Romanov's property.

"Clear," David whispered into the mike he wore as a capped tooth. The same device we all wore. It was connected to a transceiver bracketed inside our ears, much like a hearing aid, and activated by a button we wore on our collars. All wireless.

TL two-finger-waved Jonathan and me, and we soundlessly preceded him across to David. The four of us scaled the ten-foot wrought-iron fence. David first, followed by Jonathan; TL boosted me up and over, then brought up the rear.

With quiet feet, we jogged around the property, following the fence until we stood even with the greenhouse and statue garden. Remnants of yesterday's snowfall iced the ground. Thanks to the shoe-sole warmers Chapling had created, our boots melted the ice instead of crunching it.

TL pointed at Jonathan and then the ground. *Stay.* TL sprinted across the open lawn to the bushes bordering the greenhouse.

Seconds ticked by. "Clear," we heard him whisper.

David and I followed suit, bolting over open ground to TL and the bushes. Jonathan stayed behind to keep watch. David pulled a two-inch-long laser burner from his pocket. Starting at the bottom, he cut a circle in the glass, big enough for a person to crawl through. I watched him, feeling a surge of pride. Thanks to me, the laser glowed green to match the greenhouse lights. It used to be red, definitely a color someone would spot at night.

Using suction cups, he quietly lowered the clean-cut glass and then crawled through the hole. I followed, with TL staying put in the bushes as lookout. The four of us worked like bug-free software, everything in perfect rehearsed sync. A beautiful thing.

Inside the enormous, warm greenhouse, David and I scurried through perfumey flowers and more bushes until we stood on the cobblestone path. We checked our watches: 21:08:20. Ten seconds until one of the goons did his hourly stroll.

David touched one finger to his cheek, then pointed to a row of trees. *Hide.* Quickly I did as he directed while he took cover across the path.

Amazingly enough, my heartbeat steadied, my breath flowed evenly, and my stomach just existed. No erratic pulse. No choppy breath. No churning intestines. No wandering thoughts. I felt more sure, confident, and focused than I had ever felt in my whole life. Go figure. Maybe TL did know what he was doing when he put so much faith in me.

"Ah, my little bird. You make me vish my shift vas over." A guard rounded the path, a cell phone to his ear. Smirking like a stupid fool, he crossed in front of my tree. "Oh, you better stop—"

David slipped from his hiding spot, poked the guard with a numbing dart, and while soundlessly lowering him to the ground, caught the phone before it clattered across the path.

"Ah, my lovely little bird," David mimicked the goon, "zomething has come up. I vill call you back later."

It was amazing how his voice perfectly matched the bad guy's.

He dragged him the few feet to me, and together, we hid him behind the trees. Like the first guard, this one would be out for an hour.

David and I took off in a sprint down the path, past flowers, bushes, and statues, until we came to the granite Doberman statue.

Unzipping my black fanny pack, I pulled out the microsnipet locator and put on my glasses. Slowly, I ran the square device over the Doberman's legs, across its body, around its head, keeping my eyes peeled to the light indicator. It glowed a steady yellow. The light would black out when I ran it over the microsnipet. I trailed it under its belly. The light went out as I passed over the tip of its tail.

"Status," TL's voice whispered into my earpiece.

David turned from watching the path and raised his brows. I pressed the button on my collar and activated my tooth mike. "Microsnipet located. Beginning extraction now."

Tucking the locator back inside the fanny pack, I pulled

out a folding, miniature keyboard and snapped it open. It came complete with a satellite feed and one-by-four-inch monitor. Too cool.

Crouching, I studied the tiny, flat, square microsnipet. Lucky for me, it had been plastered to the surface, which meant I didn't have to break open the dog's tail to get to it. Just connect the linking wire, break the code, and download the information.

No problem. We'd know the whereabouts of Mr. Share in mere seconds.

I snapped one end of the copper linking cable to the keyboard, squeezed a dab of bonding agent to the other, then stuck it on the microsnipet. My fingers raced over the keys as I dialed the scrambler code and connected to satellite.

GOTCHA! You're in, I read on the screen. Chapling. Made me smile to think he was right here with me.

I began entering a series of standard codes, but came up against a firewall each time. I paused, focused my thoughts. Tried keying subscripts. More blocks. Worked in the opposite direction, typing synthesized indexers. Again, security barriers. Punched a list of idiosyncratic elements. Another block. What the . . .

"Status."

Jumping at TL's quiet request, I peeked at my watch. *Fifteen minutes!* I'd been at this fifteen minutes? I pressed the button on my collar. "Any second," I lied.

Okay, think, GiGi, think. Romanov owned David's dad, the most brilliant man in the world. Wouldn't it make sense that Romanov would have him create the castle's security codes? Yes, it would. Mr. Share had designed the government's security using Pascal's triangle. If he maintained the same mathematical theme, he might use quadrilateral or polynomial factoring.

My heart danced an excited little rhythm in tune to my fingers racing over the keyboard. This had to be it.

I hit the return key and—

Bingo! "I got it!"

"Shhh." David hushed me through a chuckle.

Sorry, I mouthed, grinning like a goof, watching the microsnipet info scroll onto the gray screen.

YOU GO GIRL! Chapling typed.

I stayed connected a few more minutes while he downloaded the information on the whereabouts of David's dad to our server. I disconnected from the satellite and stowed everything back in my fanny pack.

Suddenly the entire greenhouse brightened with white light, and a shrill siren went off.

I must have set off an alarm when I disconnected.

David grabbed my hand, and we took off down the path. Metal grids began unrolling from the ceiling, securing the greenhouse's glass panes and prohibiting anyone from exiting. I pumped my legs, keeping up with him. We cut through hedges and greenery, ignoring the thorny scratches, leaped over flower bushes, and slid through a spiny shrub to our entrance hole.

TL was right there, waiting for us. I glanced up to see a metal grid grinding toward us. David grabbed the back of my shirt and pants and shoved me through, then dove after me. A split second later, the grid slammed over our hole, shutting us out.

We bolted across the open frosty lawn to where Jonathan waited. In the distance we heard the pack of Dobermans as they rounded the castle and headed straight for us. TL let out a stream of curses and reached back for me. He didn't have to reach far. My fear propelled me to light speed.

Snapping and snarling, the dogs ate up the ground. Jonathan dropped to his hands and knees at the base of the wrought-iron fence. Using him as a step, David bounced onto his back and over the ten-foot-tall barrier. I went next, with TL giving me a helpful push up and over. David caught me, TL landed beside us, and Jonathan quickly scaled the fence.

The Dobermans slid to a stop, half of them barking and biting at Jonathan as he wiggled over the fence, and the other half trying to attack us through the wrought-iron spaces. With Jonathan safely on our side, we took off across the road and into the woods.

A mile later, we burst through the trees on the outskirts of an Ushbanian town, a different one from where the modeling school and hotel were located. I'd hated physical training back at the ranch, but now I was thankful for it. There was no way I'd be keeping up right now without it. I knew from our preoperations session that we would split up if something like this happened. David and I in one direction, TL in another, and Jonathan in yet another. We each wore tracking devices connected via satellite with our watches. I'd know where they were at any time, and vice versa.

TL unclipped my fanny pack, leaving me with no evidence of the mission we'd just completed, and he and Jonathan took off. Quickly, David and I removed our black face paint with wet wipes, then sprinted straight through the center of the town.

Music pounded from a nightclub four blocks up, our planned destination. Our dark clothes served two purposes, allowing us to hide in shadows, yet stylish enough for clubbing.

A police siren pierced the air. David grabbed my hand and yanked me down an alley. We ran past a dumpster and skidded to a halt when a police car pulled in the opposite end. David backed me up against the side of a building and plastered his body to mine. Our chests heaved against each other with winded breaths.

He buried his mouth against my ear. "Wrap. Your. Arms. Around. Me."

I did as he instructed, my heart hammering, keeping the police car in my peripheral vision. It slowly rolled toward us. "It's coming," I hissed, desperately trying to think of what to do next.

"Sorry," he mumbled right before crushing his mouth to mine.

TWENTY-SIX

David held his lips **firmly to mine.**

Oh my God, I'm sixteen, and I've never been kissed. Please let me be doing this right.

But . . . this was it? This was about as exciting as having my hand kissed.

The police car rolled down the alley, getting closer, keeping their spotlight pinned to us. I just hoped they were convinced we were two lovers stealing a moment alone.

Closing my eyes, I tightened my arms around David as the car slowly drove past. I concentrated on his warmth, his scent. And suddenly David was the only thing that occupied my mind. I tilted my head and opened my mouth a little bit.

"Status," TL's voice boomed in our ears.

We jumped apart. David spun away, quickly pressing the talk button on his collar. "Four blocks from club," he answered TL's interruption, all calm, as if he'd just been relaxing and reading a book.

Me? To save my life coherent thought I couldn't form. I mean, I couldn't form a coherent thought to save my life.

Squeezing my eyes shut, I half listened to them talk, replaying the kiss in my mind.

"Cop's gone."

I opened my eyes. David was looking down the dark, slushy alley. Good thing, because I had no clue what to say to him.

"I—" He stopped. "I . . ."

Oh, good God. I what? I do believe that's the best kiss I've ever had, GiGi. Or, I think we made a huge mistake, you little sixteen-year-old stupid genius.

Please don't let it be the last one.

Stepping away from the wall, I pulled my shoulders back. By God *I* would be the one to declare it a mistake, not him.

"Listen, that was a mistake. You know it, and I know it. So let's chalk it up to hormones or getting caught up in the moment or whatever." I lifted my chin and strode off down the alley like I'd seen people do in the movies.

"GiGi."

So much for my grand exit. I stopped, but didn't turn around.

"I wanted to say I was sorry because we've never talked about kissing, and I don't kiss girls unless I know for sure they want to be kissed."

But I did want to be kissed. Since the first day I saw him, I'd wanted it. I spun around. "B—"

"Like you said." He shrugged. "It was a mistake. So . . . okay. Let's get going." He breezed past me.

I turned and stared as he walked away brusquely. *Wait!*

Please! I want to change my mind. Can I change my mind? It isn't a mistake.

TWENTY-SEVEN

We spent three headachy, earsplitting hours in the club dancing on the packed floor with a strobe pulsing. The club closed at two, and we exited with the sea of bodies. Perfect cover as everyone wore black clothes like us.

Now, as we trudged into our hotel suite, TL greeted us. "Good, you're back. Let's go."

Go? What about a shower and bed? I peeked at my watch. These guys never stopped.

"Chapling decoded the info you downloaded. We know where Mr. Share is. With the alarm having been triggered, it's highly likely Romanov knows someone tapped into the microsnipet. We have to move now before Romanov relocates David's father."

David didn't blink an eye. "Let's do it."

Pivoting, I followed the guys out. David seemed amazingly calm. If I were about to rescue my dad, whom I hadn't seen in years and thought dead, I'd be a nervous wreck. "So where is he?"

"Modeling school," Jonathan answered from beside me.

Huh, I would've guessed an abandoned warehouse or

the dungeons in Romanov's castle. That's where the bad guys hid good guys in the movies.

Bypassing the elevator, TL opened the stairwell door, and we each passed through. "According to the blueprints, there's a steel-walled room off Romanov's office on the third floor. I assumed it was a weapons room. Makes sense that's where Mr. Share is."

"So it's still a weapons room." I took a couple of steps down. "Because David's dad is the ultimate weapon."

Jonathan stopped, and I ran straight into his hard back. In the cramped stairwell, all three guys turned to stare at me. *What?*

"You're right." TL spoke first. "Never thought about it that way. He *is* the ultimate weapon."

Okay. Nothing like saying something profound to get everyone's attention. Although it only made sense. Mr. Share could hack his way into anything. He could squirm through the military's system and set off nuclear bombs.

Wait a minute. So could I.

A chill raced through my body at the evil I was capable of doing. No wonder the good guys recruited me. But was I at risk of being kidnapped like David's dad? For my brain? TL said the IPNC had kept tabs on me since I was a child. Had all the bad guys out there in the world done so, too?

Gulp.

We continued descending the hotel's stairs, rounding the second floor to the first. "Why am I with you? You don't need me to rescue Mr. Share."

Jonathan opened the exit door, sending in the icy night. "We're not leaving you alone in the suite. Plus we need a lookout."

"Oh." I tucked my gloved hands into my jacket pockets.

On foot we trekked four cobblestoned blocks and then

cut through the woods to the modeling school. At this early-morning hour, Prost, Ushbania, sat dark and empty. Yellow streetlights provided the only illumination. It was a cute little town. Like if a shepherd and his flock wandered across the street, it wouldn't surprise me a bit.

The modeling school stood three stories high between two other brick buildings. A street ran in front and a small stream along the back.

The four of us lay belly down on the other side of the stream, staring across at the buildings. Behind us stretched miles of wooded hills that eventually led to Romanov's castle.

TL spread leaves over my back and legs. He pointed at me, then the ground. *Stay.* He waved Jonathan to the right, David to the left, and TL slipped back into the woods. My job in all this? To lie on the cold, damp ground, camouflaged by leaves, watching the back side of the modeling school. Of course if I saw someone, I would press my collar talk button, activating my tooth mike, and notify my team.

Jonathan and David appeared moments later on the other side of the stream, creeping down opposite ends of the back alley. TL popped up on the roof. I did a double take. Jeez, the man moved quick.

He disappeared into the shadows, but I knew what he was doing. "Clear," he whispered seconds later. He'd disabled the security system.

David and Jonathan sprinted to the back door. Kneeling, David picked the lock and the two of them slid inside. TL signaled me from the roof. *Five minutes.*

They'd be five minutes. Shielding my watch, I pressed the indiglo button, confirming the time: 3:20:03. I knew TL well enough to know that at precisely 3:25:03 they would reappear at my side.

With a quiet sigh, I ran my gaze over the dark modeling school, studying the windows, hoping to see a flicker of light, a movement of shadows. They were too good, though. They'd be in and out before anyone was the wiser.

3:21:15.

Little under four minutes to go. A frosty breeze blew past, sending leaves rolling across the ground. I fought the urge to shiver and pull my coat tighter around me, concentrating instead on keeping very still. I thought about a nice cup of hot chocolate when we got back. Followed by a cinnamon lollipop. Oooh, gonna be good.

3:22:31.

TL would want to leave for the States as soon as possible, though. Hot chocolate or not. It made sense. Who'd want to hang out in Ushbania after stealing back a man worth millions of dollars? Not I.

3:23:17.

Did they have him yet? Had David been reunited with his dad? They were probably hugging at this very second, sharing a moment. Wished I could be there to see it.

3:24:05.

Oh, yeah. In under a minute they'd be back. We'd be off through the woods and on a plane to the States. Any second now I'd be meeting Mr. Share.

A twig snapped behind me, and I let out a relieved breath, then immediately caught it. Wait a minute, they wouldn't be coming up from behind.

"Don't do anyzing stupid."

I froze.

"Get up."

Carefully I pushed to my hands and knees, my heart banging so hard it'd probably break a rib. With my hands raised above my head, I slowly turned around. Two giant goons stood with feet braced apart, aiming matching guns at my head.

One grabbed my arm and yanked me toward him. He pressed a gun to my side, and we charged off into the woods.

I yanked back. "Helllp!"

The goon behind me shoved me forward. "Quiet."

They dragged me around trees and over downed limbs. *This isn't supposed to he happening!* I dug my heels in. *"Helllp!"*

He jabbed the gun into my ribs. "Ooowww!"

"Shut up."

I hit a pile of muddy leaves and slid to my butt.

He jerked me up. "Stupid girl."

Wait, I should scream. Surely by now my team was outside the modeling school and would hear me. I took a breath, ready to let loose with a loud one.

"Don't"—the goon ground the gun into my ribs—"even zink about it."

I chanced a quick glance over my shoulder, couldn't even see the dim lights of the buildings. What if my team was still inside the modeling school? They wouldn't even know I'd been kidnapped. Of all the time for them to be running late, this was not it.

"GiGi," TL whispered through my earpiece.

My earpiece! I'd forgotten I was wearing it. I tried not to react to TL's voice so as not to tip off the goons.

"Don't fight them," he continued. "You're wearing a tracking device. We know exactly where you are."

That's right. Under my cotton shirt I still wore the freckle on my neck from Romanov's party, and my watch linked via satellite. The whole IPNC knew my GPS coordinates.

"We'll get you back safely." David. His voice made my breath hitch. "I promise."

The goon jerked me from the woods and across the street to a waiting black sedan. He opened the car door. I tugged at his grip. "Nooo."

He shoved me inside, pushing in behind me. The other goon took the front seat, and the car peeled out.

I scooted over as far as I could. Where were they taking me? When would my team find me?

The goon grabbed my wrist and tore off the watch.

Ow! "Hey . . ." That hurt.

He rolled down the window and hurled out the watch. I watched in shock as it sailed into the night. How'd he know to take it off of me? Were these GPS watches standard for both good guys and bad?

Leaning across, the goon briskly frisked me, running his hands clumsily along my legs, arms, front, and back.

Shoving me over, he secured my wrists behind my back with industrial tape. He pulled a black hood from his pocket and fit it over my head.

He and the other goon exchanged words in Ushbanian. The car cut a corner, and I slid off the leather seat onto the floor. He yanked me back up. A few seconds later, he began a one-sided conversation, presumably on a cell phone. Probably talking to Romanov about what to do with me. I heard him say Jade January. Well, they knew who I was.

Underneath the hood, I closed my eyes. Somehow the darkness of my lids didn't bother me as much as the blackness of the cloth.

Calm down, GiGi. Calm down. Think code. That always settles you.

<ILNI= 1 S:%-11-:oo=ISLI>

<1/foo.hlt: 15-30#@//lmt>

Unfortunately it didn't work this time. I sniffed. *I won't cry,* I promised myself as a tear slid down my cheek.

In, then out. In, then out. I concentrated on my breathing, trying to stay as calm as possible. Trying not to imagine all the things they might do to me before my team rescued me.

I still wore my tracking freckle and ear transceiver. With my hands tied, I couldn't access my collar talk button, but at least I would hear my team if they spoke. At least they knew my coordinates.

It could be a whole lot worse.

That's what I told myself. Convinced myself of, really.

The car slowed to a stop. Based on the time we'd driven, I'd say we were probably in the country at Romanov's castle.

Gripping my arm, the goon pulled me from the car into the frozen night. He led me along a path, and we entered a warm, musty building. We descended 102 steps. I counted them like TL taught me. *Be aware of everything,* he'd said.

Something metal creaked in front of me, like a door being opened. The goon ripped the hood from my head and shoved me forward, slamming the door behind me.

I gritted my teeth in anger, pleased to feel that emotion over fear. They didn't have to be so rough. I'd go on my own if they'd ask.

Dimly lit, the square room was approximately twenty by twenty feet. One single metal chair sat dead center on the cement floor. No way I'd sit in it. That's where the bad guys tied the good guys while torturing information from them. The drain under the chair probably made for ease in washing away blood. Although no red remnants stained the sterile room.

Where was this place? The dungeons of Romanov's

castle? A deserted building? Maybe they'd driven me around to make me think we were going someplace else, and we were actually still at the modeling school.

Starting in the corner, I paced the perimeter. With my hands still tied, I could only visually inspect the cinder-block, windowless walls. I didn't see any cameras. Not to say they weren't hidden somewhere. Surely they wouldn't put me in here without monitoring me.

Minutes rolled by and I continued pacing.

The door unbolted, and I spun around right as a goon tore a hood off someone and shoved him inside. David!

Relief hit me hard, and tears burst free. The bravery I'd talked myself into, the irritation at being roughly handled, gushed free. Only euphoria at not being alone and comfort at seeing someone familiar flooded my senses.

The goon slammed the door, closing David and me up. With his hands tied behind his back, he covered the short distance between us. No one had ever looked so welcoming as he did at this very moment.

He pressed his cheek to mine. "Shhh . . ."

I sniffed, but more tears fell. All the fear at being kidnapped and not knowing what would happen flowed from my soul. All the warm support of his cheek against mine made me want to sob. Yet sobbing was the absolute last thing either of us needed.

Questions ping-ponged through my brain as I slowly regained composure. What's he doing here? Did the bad guys get TL and Jonathan, too? Where's David's dad?

Sniffing, I wiped my cheek on my shoulder. David leaned back with a slight curve to his lips, which made me smile. "What happen—"

David placed his lips against my ear. "Stay in character," he murmured. "Not sure how much they know.

They're watching and listening. Remember that. Got caught on purpose. Didn't want you alone. Help's on the way."

Got caught on purpose. Didn't want you alone.

My stomach fluttered at his meaningful words. Shifting, I pressed my lips to his jaw. *This might be the last kiss of my life,* I thought, taking in his warmth, enjoying his stubble brushing my face.

The door unbolted, and we reluctantly moved away from each other.

Petrov, the GQ guy from the party, came into the room. He'd been so nice. I couldn't imagine him harming anyone.

Romanov followed, and dread settled in. He didn't strike me as the type to play nice. Quietly, he approached us, coming to a stop right in front of me. He studied me through black, soulless eyes.

Keeping my back against the wall, I fought the urge to fidget, to swallow, to hide my eyes from his evil gaze. The longer he scrutinized me, the more aware I became of my thundering heart and irregular breaths.

He lifted his hand, and David took a step forward. "Leave her alone."

"I vill"—Romanov didn't take his eyes off me—"not hurt her."

He caressed a finger down my cheek. His creepy softness scared me more than his goons' brute force. "I do not vant her touched. Such beauty should be vorshipped."

The do-not-touch order gave me a flicker of faith.

Romanov brushed a thumb over my black eye. "Seems like my statue did great damage to your delicateness."

He pressed my black eye just enough to make me cringe, killing off the flicker of faith. He knew exactly what he was doing.

"A model who knows how to extract information from a microsnipet. Hmm . . ." Romanov patted my cheek. "So tell me, how long have you been a spy?"

"I don't know what you're talking about."

His lips curved into a creepy smile. "Ah, you vill tell me in time."

In time? How long did he plan on keeping me?

He turned and strolled from the room, Petrov following. They closed and bolted the door, and I blew out a long, shaky breath.

David came to me. "You okay?"

Okay? I was far from okay. Kidnapped, locked in a dungeon, shoved around by goons. No telling what came next. I nodded, though. "You?"

"Fine."

Roughly ten minutes later, the door unbolted again, sending nausea straight to my mouth. Nalani stepped in. Not her, too. I really liked her.

"Come quick," she whispered.

TWENTY-EIGHT

I glanced at David.

What if this was a trap? What if Nalani worked for a different bad group and was leading us straight to them? What if she was only pretending to help us as part of some twisted game Romanov was playing?

David nodded. "It's all right. She's one of us."

She's one of us? Why hadn't he told me?

"I'll tell you later," he said, reading my mind.

With a pocketknife, Nalani sliced the duct tape binding our hands. We followed her silently from the dungeon through a maze of narrow, dark tunnels. Jogging soundlessly, barely breathing, making as little noise as possible.

We came to a slim, steel door. She dug a key from her pants pocket and quickly unlocked it. Frosty air gushed in as we rushed out. The three of us bolted over frozen leaves and dirt toward bordering woods.

I peeked over my shoulder but didn't recognize the house. Small, neat, and tidy. Who would ever guess it contained a dungeon? Behind the house, in the distance, loomed the castle. We were on Romanov's property.

We sprinted into the dark woods. TL and Jonathan emerged from the shadows, and I nearly leaped for joy.

Nalani gave David and me quick hugs. "Be safe. I'll see you in a while." She dashed off in the opposite direction.

Leading the way, TL ran through the woods, and we followed, with Jonathan in the rear. A gazillion questions zinged my brain. Where were we going? Where was David's dad? Who was Nalani? What about Romanov and his goons? Had David known Nalani would rescue us?

We emerged from the woods and came to a skidding stop.

There stood Romanov, seven goons looming alongside him.

Uh-oh.

They must have heard us because they all turned at once. TL, Jonathan, and David moved lightning quick before I blinked or Romanov's men registered what was going on. Fists and feet shot out in calculated, high-flying kicks and swings. Bones cracked. Blood flew. Men grunted. Within seconds, three goons lay passed out on the road, or maybe dead, and my team moved on to the next set.

Snapping from my shocked trance, I quickly recalled self-defense training and ran toward the mob. Bruiser popped into my mind. For the first time in my life, I wished I was a small, redheaded, freckled girl with killer fighting capabilities.

In my peripheral vision, I caught Romanov slinking back into the woods. *Wimp.*

Petrov charged me. I spun and roundhoused him in the stomach. His face registered disbelief as he stumbled backward.

That's right, buddy, disbelieve this.

I stalked his stumbling body, gaining ground, and

uppercut him in the nose. Blood and curses gushed from him. His shocked expression transformed to squinty eyes and hard jaw. Like he was thinking, *Zere's no way zis female vill vin.*

Yeah? Well, he'd never fought a possessed genius until now.

I chopped him in the Adam's apple, ignoring the popping sound, then whipped around and smashed my heel into his kneecap. Gagging, he grabbed hold of his throat and fell to his knees.

Scowling at his hunched form, I circled behind him. I put him in a headlock, my right arm around his throat and left pressing the back of his neck. He jerked against my hold, clawing at my jacketed arm, wheezing for breath. Seconds later, he went limp.

I released him and stepped back, resisting the urge to dust my hands in victory. Ready to take on my next opponent, I glanced up. TL, Jonathan, and David stood with their feet braced apart and arms folded, watching me. On the ground around them sprawled Ushbanian goons in various passed-out positions.

My team broke into matching grins and applauded.

Smiling in return, I gave in to the urge to dust my hands, and they burst out laughing.

Just then a windowless, black van came barreling down the dirt road. Great, more bad guys.

TL started toward it. "Ride's here."

My shoulders drooped in relief. That meant an airplane back to the States was mere hours away. I was actually excited about getting on a plane. Go figure.

Stepping around Petrov, I followed the guys toward the van. Fatigue hit me hard, and my boots dragged in the dirt. I'd had little or no sleep since leaving California.

Hard to believe so much had happened in the span of four days.

From the driver's seat, Nalani nodded as I passed by. I tripped as I did a double take, which made her smile. I bet she was the insider TL had told us about.

TL opened the back door. "Let's go."

I climbed in ahead of the guys, expecting to see Mr. Share, but empty cargo space met me instead. I took a seat on the hard floor, as did the guys, and Nalani drove off. A thick screen separated her from us, and I barely saw her profile.

No one spoke, so I kept quiet, too, but jeez, I wanted answers.

David sat across from me, his eyes closed, head lolling in pre-sleep. Beside me, Jonathan did the same. Next to David, TL dialed the satellite phone. A few seconds later, he began speaking in hushed tones. I made out the words *plane, four people, twenty minutes,* and *coffin.*

Coffin? Oh, no, did that mean Mr. Share was dead? I shot a quick glance across the van, but David hadn't moved a muscle. He would've told me by now, wouldn't he? Yeah, right, not like we'd had any time to talk.

How awful for him. To have just been reunited with his dad only to discover he was now dead.

I looked at TL, hoping to learn something, anything, but he'd already ended the call and closed his eyes as well. How anyone could sleep in the back of a noisy, bumpy cargo van was beyond me. But I shut my eyes anyway . . .

"GiGi." Someone nudged my leg. "We gotta move."

My lids popped open in dead-asleep-to-wide-awake alertness. "How long—"

"An hour." David knelt beside me. The van shifted as TL and Jonathan jumped out.

I gripped David's forearm. "Is your dad okay? I heard TL say 'coffin.'"

David shook his head. "That's how we're smuggling him out of the country."

"Oh." I smiled. "I'm glad. Wait, can he survive in a coffin that long?"

"In our coffin he can. Plenty of oxygen, snacks, and water. He'll be fine. Come on, we gotta move."

We hopped from the van into a dawning, icy morning. A forest surrounded us. We were, literally, out in the middle of nowhere. A small, wooden shack stood off to the right, hidden among towering pines. A limo and a hearse sat alongside the shack, looking so out of place I almost laughed.

We crossed the short distance to the shack. David opened the creaky door, and the van cranked its engine. I whipped around.

Nalani. She waved as she drove off through a rough-cut path.

"Who is she?"

"Tell you later." He ushered me inside. "We've got only five minutes."

Already dressed, TL passed us on the way out. Jonathan followed, tucking in his shirt. They'd changed back into their bodyguard and modeling agent clothes.

Except for our suitcases heaped in the middle, a camping stove in the corner, and a small window above it, the dark, wood shack stood dusty and empty. "What is this place?"

"Safe house."

Safe house. Hmm. There was probably more to it than there appeared to be. Maybe a hidden hatch leading to an underground passage. Or a secret panel that opened onto a cache of tucked-away weapons. The whole structure was probably wired with microfilters and thermal thirystors. My pulse kicked in at the techie possibilities.

A man emerged from the shadows, and I jumped.

He smiled and held out his hand. "Mike Share."

My jaw dropped. "Oh, my goodness." I took his hand. "It's so great to meet you. I'm GiGi."

He pumped my hand. "I know."

David threw open my biggest suitcase, snatched the first thing he put his hands on, and threw it to me. "Hurry. You can use the bathroom."

Bathroom? I gazed in the direction he indicated. Sure enough, a door sat seamlessly in the wall. I hurried over and inside and came to an abrupt stop.

Yuck.

A filthy toilet, minus the seat, occupied one corner. Dirty water filled the bowl. A grimy sink stood beside it. Above that hung a mirror layered so thick in dust it prohibited me from seeing myself. No tub. And it smelled like . . . well, you can guess what it smelled like.

"Hurry," David shouted.

I jumped into action, quickly changing, touching as little of the bathroom as possible.

With my old clothes in hand, I opened the door. David had already put on his photographer's clothes. He took one look at my low-rise jeans and blue turtleneck and dug in the suitcase. He tossed me a pair of black, chunky-heeled boots and a black leather jacket.

I threw him my old clothes. "Why are we changing? The mission's over."

"Missions are never over until we return home." He shoved everything back inside the suitcases. "When you assume a new identity, you maintain that identity until you're back at home base. In case some last-second thing goes wrong."

"Makes sense."

While he zipped the suitcases closed, I rapidly finished off my outfit.

We grabbed the luggage and bolted out the door toward the limo and hearse.

David and his dad exchanged a long, hard hug. Then Mr. Share climbed into the back of the hearse.

After throwing the baggage in the trunk of the limo, we joined TL and Jonathan in the back. The limo pulled off, and I closed my eyes with a sigh.

Almost over. Nearly home. So many unanswered questions.

A soft buzzing made me open my eyes. Across from me, TL and Jonathan were shaving with electric razors. Beside me, David brushed his teeth.

TL handed me a small gray bag. "Get in modeling role. Wear sunglasses to hide your eye."

I unzipped it. A butterscotch lollipop lay right on top. My heart warmed with love. How sweet—they packed my candy.

Makeup and toiletries filled the pouch. I rifled through, found a mirror, and took a peek. Sheesh, what a mess. I pulled out a wet wipe and began washing my face.

Whoever thought I'd be riding in a limo with three guys, getting ready, like sharing a bathroom or something?

We pulled up to the international airport, stepped from the cozy, warm limo, and it was like nothing had ever happened. Jonathan whipped out his cell phone, TL stuck stoically to my side, and David strutted cockily behind. I led the way, strolling through the terminal, head up and shoulders back.

"Your autograph?"

Smiling down at the young boy, I took his pad of paper and pen and scrawled *Jade January*. He had no idea who I was. But with my entourage, I sure seemed like someone famous.

The airport announced our flight. With a good-bye wave to the boy, we made our way onto the plane.

"Who's Nalani?" I whispered to David after we took our first-class seats. "And what about Romanov? What happened to him?"

David shook his head with a yawn, closed his eyes, and lay back. "Later."

I peered across the aisle to where Jonathan and TL sat. They'd already reclined their seat backs. With a resigned sigh, I shut my eyes.

David shifted in his seat. He slid his arm over the top of mine and we linked fingers. "Breeeaaathe," he muttered sleepily.

Breeeaaathe. He was worried about my fear of flying. How sweet. I lowered my head to his shoulder, cradling our intertwined arms between us, and cuddled into his warmth.

Seconds later, he rested his cheek on my head. "Mmmm . . ."

Mmmm, indeed.

TWENTY-NINE

Sixteen hours later, our limo pulled up in front of the ranch with Mr. Share's hearse behind us.

David leaped from the limo before it came to a full stop and sprinted to the hearse.

I stepped out with Jonathan and TL following. We all still wore our mission clothes.

David flung open the back of the hearse and disappeared inside. Seconds later, he emerged with his father. Mr. Share squeezed David's shoulder and said something. David laughed. The sound brought a smile to my face. I hadn't seen him so genuinely happy in a while.

His hand still on David's shoulder, Mr. Share approached us. He and David didn't look anything alike. Exact opposites really. Mr. Share stood a little shorter than David and had blond hair instead of brown. David must favor his mother.

TL popped the trunk on the limo. "How was the coffin?"

"Soft jazz, Cheetos, sweet tea, a down pillow, full

night's rest." Mr. Share smiled. "All my favorite things. It's been ten years since I've had them. I can't complain."

His coffin ride sounded more comfortable than our first-class seats.

I was dying to ask him about the last ten years of his life. But TL had told me Mr. Share was not allowed to say anything or access a computer until IPNC officials had debriefed and cleared him.

Mr. Share closed his eyes and lifted his face to the sun. He drew in a slow, deep breath.

I watched him, wondering what it would be like to be locked away for ten years without fresh air, the sun, the rain. To sit at a computer year in and year out and steal money for a terrorist. It was amazing that he hadn't gone insane from the isolation. Thoughts of David must have kept him going.

TL grabbed two suitcases from the limo's trunk. "We'll pile the luggage in the hall and head straight to the computer lab."

My teammates would be home from school in a little while. The thought excited me. I realized that I'd missed them.

Jonathan and David each took a duffel bag. I reached for a suitcase at the same time as Mr. Share.

"Sorry." I laughed.

He smiled at me. "ST and BIR," he whispered, as he quickly picked up another piece of luggage and strode toward the front door.

ST and BIR?

Scrunching my brows, I studied his back, slowly following everyone inside. I tried to catch Mr. Share's eyes to silently ask him what he meant, but he wouldn't look at me.

Minutes later, we entered Chapling's and my lab. Chapling's and *my* lab. I loved saying that.

Chapling stood at the coffeepot, pouring himself what I felt sure was his billionth cup of the day.

He glanced up as we strode in. "Hey!" He caught sight of Mr. Share. "Mike!" Chapling put the pot down and hurried over. "Wow!"

Chuckling, Mr. Share leaned down and hugged him. "Hey, Chap, been a long time. You look just the same."

"Oh, yeah. Yeahyeahyeahyeahyeah. Still short and redheaded."

Everyone laughed.

Chapling gave me a quick hug. "Missed you."

I squeezed him back. "I missed you, too."

He waved everyone in. "Come in. Welcomewelcomewelcome."

We all scooted in.

Chapling wiggled up onto his stool. "So where's this famous chip you programmed with all the government's information?"

Mr. Share leaned against the table bisecting the lab. "It's in David's butt."

David and I exchanged confused glances.

Chapling burst out laughing. "It's in his what?"

"You heard me right." Mr. Share nodded.

TL shook his head. "I don't understand."

Mr. Share turned to David. "Know that tiny scar on your backside?"

David nodded.

"That's where I had it surgically inserted over a decade ago."

Nobody uttered a sound. Probably because they were thinking the exact same thing as me. What the . . . ?

"You mean"—David laughed—"I've been carrying around the key to our nation's security in my rump?"

"Yep."

"Man, Dad, you're a loon."

Mr. Share shrugged. "I have my moments. So, if GiGi will excuse us, the doctor should be here any second. We can finally get it out, transfer the information, and then lock it away for good."

"Well," I glanced at David, dropping my gaze to his backside. "Good luck."

He shook his head with a chuckle. "Thanks."

TL followed me from the lab. We made our way through the ranch's underground hallways, past the locked doors that still remained a mystery to me.

At the elevator, TL stopped me. "I'm proud to say I've been on a mission with you. You not only met my expectations but far exceeded them. You've proven time and time again how valuable you are to this team. Don't ever question or forget that."

Pride swelled inside me. TL rarely gave accolades unless he really meant them. So when he did, it made it even that much more special. "Thank you."

He nodded.

My brain replayed his praise over and over again as I rode the elevator to the main floor. We parted ways in the hallway, he to his office and me to the girls' bedroom. Amazing how many changes I'd been through over the past couple of months. Emotionally and physically.

I never imagined I'd turn out this way.

I entered the girls' bedroom, heading straight for my old dinged-up suitcase. Time to unpack. Time to make this place my real home.

Beaker sat cross-legged in the corner with Wirenut.

She'd dyed her hair blue while I was gone. They were unpacking their book bags. They must have just gotten home.

I smiled at them both. "Hi." Boy, it felt good to see them.

Wirenut glanced up and returned my smile. "Welcome home, GiGi. Everyone missed you."

"Thanks."

"Nice shiner." Beaker smirked.

Okay, apparently everyone missed me *but* her. I didn't take offense, though. Her smirk was her way of saying she'd missed me.

I wanted to tell them everything about my mission, but I wasn't allowed. They knew that and didn't ask for details. TL would tell them what he wanted them to know.

Wirenut nodded to my dresser. "Your new glasses came in. They look *a lot* better than those weird wire ones you've been wearing."

I made a face at him and he laughed.

Bruiser rushed into the room, closing the door behind her. Her T-shirt read JUST TRY ME. She gave me a quick hug. "Glad you're back." She held out her hands. "You're not going to believe what I just overheard. TL's on the phone with somebody, and I heard him say, 'What do you mean the Specialists lost funding?'"

THIRTY

I stayed rooted to my spot, one hand hovering over my suit-case, staring at Bruiser.

The Specialists lost funding? What the . . . ? It didn't make any sense. "I don't understand."

Bruiser shrugged. "I don't know. He's arguing with someone right now. I heard him say, 'Where are the kids supposed to go? We're family.'"

Wirenut pushed to his feet, knocking over his and Beaker's chemistry experiment. "Darn right we're family. First one I've had, and I'm not losing it." He strode to the door. "I'm finding out what's going on."

Beaker jumped up. "Wait for me."

"Me, too." Bruiser hurried after them.

I followed behind at a numb, slower shuffle, too stunned to do much of anything else. Where would I go? What would I do? I could go back to East Iowa University and finish up my studies. But somehow I couldn't picture myself back in that old lifestyle.

My future was different now. *I* was different now. For the first time in my life, I belonged somewhere. People here relied on me and needed me. I needed each and every one of them, too.

Even Beaker and her sour moods.

Tears welled up in my eyes as their faces flashed across my brain. Chapling's fuzzy red head and caffeine-induced hyperactivity. Bruiser's innocent freckles and kick-butt moves. Wirenut's goatee and electronics brilliance. Mystic's football neck and peaceful aura. Beaker's Goth clothes and chemistry tubes. Parrot's Native American heritage and multilinguistic tongue. Jonathan's eye patch and physical training. TL's unending patience.

And David . . .

I caught my breath on an overwhelming feeling of loss. This hodgepodge of a group was my family. I couldn't say good-bye. I *wouldn't* say good-bye.

Wirenut tapped on TL's door.

"Enter."

"What's happening?" Mystic whispered from down the hall.

Bruiser put her finger to her lips and motioned him and Parrot to join us where we stood.

Wirenut pushed TL's door open and stepped inside. We crowded in behind him. "We would like to know what's going on."

Sitting behind his desk, TL leaned back in his chair and crossed his arms. He made eye contact with each of us, slowly moving from one to another. "I take it one of you overheard me on the phone."

"Me, sir." Bruiser raised her hand.

TL nodded, accepting. "We lost our funding as a result of the government's budget cuts." He closed his eyes briefly, then reopened them. Sorrow and devastation contorted his face.

I stared in stunned amazement, unable to grasp the emotion he displayed. This from a man who was always in control.

"I'm sorry." He lowered his chair to the floor. "I'm truly sorry. I'll call an official meeting in one hour after I know more." He picked up the phone. "Close the door on your way out."

We shuffled into the hall and just stood there. Silently. Our shoulders weighted with worry. I felt sure the same question replayed in everyone's brain.

What's going to happen to us?

With a sigh, Wirenut turned away first. The rest of us trudged behind, back down the hall to the girls' bedroom. Nobody uttered a sound as we sprawled across the beds, fixing our gazes on the carpet, walls, ceilings, or furniture.

Silent moments ticked by, broken only by someone's sigh.

"This sucks." Bruiser interrupted the quiet.

Parrot flopped from his stomach to his back. "You got that right."

"Not like TL doesn't want us." Beaker heaved a frustrated breath. "It's money, right? If we could find money, we'd be set."

Mystic shoved a pillow under his head. "Hey, Wirenut, feel like going back to your old ways? Break into a bank or two."

Wirenut chuckled halfheartedly. "No, I'm not going back to my old ways."

If we could find money, we'd be set. Beaker's words echoed through my brain as I lay beside Wirenut, staring at the ceiling.

ST and BIR.

I jackknifed up, realization slapping me in the face.

Shooting off the bed, I raced from the room and down the hall to the elevator. Faintly, I heard the others call after me.

Shaking with anticipation, I placed my hand on the globe-light print scan. While the laser skimmed my fingers and palm, dizziness waved through me.

Oh, no, not now.

The door opened, and I staggered inside. *Hold on, GiGi, you're almost there.*

As I plastered my body to the wall, the elevator tilted, and I squeezed my eyes shut. *Don't pass out.*

Three years ago I did. From my rapid-fore processes. The doctor said my brain worked too fast for my body. I felt that familiar trance coming on now.

The elevator opened, and I stumbled out. Right into David's arms.

"GiGi, you okay?"

With a jerky nod, I pushed away. "C'puter."

"Wha—"

Shaking my head, I stumbled a few feet toward Chapling's and my lab. The hallway morphed to a stretched blur. *Don't black out. Hold on.*

David slipped his arm under my knees and swooshed me off the ground. He sprinted down the hall with me bouncing lightly in his arms.

At the lab's door, he lowered me and, holding me tight, punched in the code. I dropped my forehead to his shoulder, my brain triple-timing, fighting the urge to give in and pass out.

He carried me across the lab to my computer, slid me into the seat, and placed my hands on the keyboard.

My fingers took on a life of their own, racing over the keys, translating my cerebrum's processes.

I sat hypnotized by the scrolling screen, letting my body and brain lead the way.

Seconds passed, or maybe minutes. David slipped a lollipop in my mouth—yum, mango—then glasses on my nose. The screen cleared, and immediately my fatigue lifted. Like I'd gotten a shot of caffeine.

"Oh, smartgirlsmartgirl," Chapling mumbled from behind me.

"What's she doing?"

"Ohyeahohyeahohyeah. Gogogogogo."

"Chapling?"

"Oh, sorry." Chapling giggled. "She's worming her way through ST and BIR."

"ST and BIR?"

"Security Trust and Banking International Records."

"That's not legal."

"Shhh."

David cursed. "She's not stealing, is she?"

"Nonononono. Nothing like that. She's looking for Romanov's money. Shhh, let her work."

"Exactly what I was hoping she would do," Mr. Share whispered. I hadn't even realized he'd come in.

They stopped talking as I wound through one account to the next. Spiraling through special-interest funds, jumping from government finances to private. With each successful hop, my crowded brain cleared a little, popping focus and energy back into place.

Aaahhh. Excitement jolted through my veins. There you are, you sneaky little weasel.

Couple more keystrokes and I clicked print. "Let's go."

THIRTY-ONE

TL closed the conference-room door. With a contented curve to his lips, he swept his gaze around the packed room. The Specialists Teams One and Two, Jonathan, Chapling, and Mr. Share all crowded in. I stood along the sidewall between Parrot and Mystic.

"By now, all of you know the government pulled our funding in recent budget cuts. I don't think I have to say how much this place means to me. To all of us." TL cleared his throat. "Unbeknownst to me, GiGi took it upon herself to find the needed monies."

Everyone turned and looked at me, and my stomach turned one huge flip.

"Romanov Schalmosky made a career of stealing. Not only from the United States, but from other countries as well. He took technology, money." TL glanced at Mr. Share. "People, too. GiGi found Romanov's money and deposited it back in the accounts of the rightful owners."

The entire room broke into cheers, and I grinned, literally, from ear to ear. I glanced across the room to where Mr. Share stood, and he winked at me.

TL held his hands up for silence. "We've notified everyone that she's found and returned their money. And they, in turn, gave us a generous percentage. The Specialists are back in action. We're private now, though. No more government funding. We work for whoever hires us. So let's call it a day and celebrate. Everyone meet up top in the common area in ten. We got a party going on."

Everyone cheered again, catcalling and whooping.

Mystic poked me in the ribs. "Go, GiGi."

Parrot bumped my shoulder with his. "That's our genius girl."

Smiling, I bumped him back.

Specialist Team Two passed me on their way out, punching my shoulder and thanking me.

Jonathan bear-hugged me. "I'm so proud of you."

Chapling did some sort of jig. "Smartgirl, smartgirl."

TL took my hand and clasped it warmly between both of his. Like he'd done so many times over the months to calm, comfort, and reassure me. "I knew you'd fit in."

He was right. I did fit in. More than I ever thought possible.

Mr. Share kissed my cheek. "Young lady, I don't know what to say to you. Thank you is too small to express my gratitude. If it weren't for you, there's no telling who would own me now. I owe you my life. If you ever need anything, you just ask. I'll do everything in my power to make your every wish come true."

The meaningfulness in his voice and words left me humbly mute. I *had* saved his life, hadn't I? "And thank you. ST and BIR?" I whispered.

He winked. "I knew where Romanov's money was. And I thought that a computer whiz with access to a keyboard could use that information."

"Will I see you again?"

"Perhaps. I have a series of debriefings to go through. I've been gone a long time. A known terrorist has kept me prisoner for the past ten years. The United States government has a lot of questions for me. I'll be relocated soon with a new identity."

"What about David?"

"We'll see each other occasionally." Mr. Share kissed my cheek again, and then he leaned back and studied my face. "Gosh," he said, chuckling. "You look just like your mother."

I looked just like my . . . ? What . . . ? My mother . . . ? H-how . . . how did he know what my mother looked like?

With a quick pinch to my chin, he headed from the room.

My file. He'd probably seen my file.

My team shuffled in, surrounding me. I stood in the center, looking at each of their silly smiles. What were they up to now?

"GROUP HUUUG!" they yelled, and collided together, smooshing me in the middle.

We laughed and giggled and jabbed one another.

"Okay, okay, break it up." David wedged us apart. "Scat. I want a moment alone with the woman who saved the day."

"Ooohhh," my team teased. "He wants a moment alooone."

David chuckled and waved them off. "Get outta here."

We watched them file out and close the door.

I smiled. "I really missed them."

"Ya know, it's neat that you all have chosen to go by your code names all the time."

Yeah, it was. "Why doesn't Team One?"

David shrugged. "Don't know. We just don't."

They had their matching Specialists T-shirts, and we had our nicknames.

Slowly, David moved in, backing me up against the wall, until we stood toe-to-toe, our faces only inches from each other. My normal, happy, pitter-patter pulse revved to hyperdrive mode, and my stomach nose-dived to the floor.

"Smell good you." I shook my head. "I mean, you smell good." I groaned. "Did I actually say that out loud?"

His dark eyes crinkled with amusement. "You're nervous right now. Do you know how I know you're nervous right now?"

Swallowing, I shook my head.

"Because you always mix up your words when you get nervous."

"Oh."

David tapped my forehead. "I think smart chicks are cool."

He'd said the exact same thing back at East Iowa University.

"So, smart chick, I just wanted you to know you did a great job."

"Thanks," I croaked.

Smiling, he pressed a kiss to my cheek, linked fingers with me, and led me from the conference room. "Come on. TL's waiting."

My coherence slowly returned as we made our way through the underground corridors, past the mysterious locked doors. "What's behind all those?"

"You know I can't tell you. Everyone finds out when TL wants them to."

"Well, that's a bummer."

David laughed.

"Hey, what about Nalani? And Romanov, too. What happened to him?"

We came to the elevator. David punched in his code and placed his hand on the fingerprint-identification panel. We stepped inside.

"Nalani apprehended Romanov. He's not expected to live long. He'll die in custody."

It took a moment for that to sink in. "Who is she?"

David folded his arms across his chest and leaned back against the elevator's wall. I enjoyed a delicious second of staring at his tanned biceps, curved out from his white T-shirt.

"Don't say a word about this to anyone, okay?"

I nodded, peeling my gaze away from his muscles.

"Nalani's TL's wife."

My jaw dropped. "Shut up. Are you serious?"

"Yep."

"Wow. That's huge."

"She works for the IPNC. She's what we call a preoperator. She goes in before the actual mission and gathers intelligence. Cements herself within the opposing organization."

"That's so dangerous."

"She worked for Romanov almost two years." David lifted off the wall when the elevator stopped.

"Unbelievable." What dedication she had to her job. "Why aren't she and TL living together?"

David shrugged. "Don't know the details. This mission was the first time I met her."

"Why didn't anyone tell me her identity?"

"TL and IPNC were concerned that she might have defected. But obviously she's still on our side."

"Will we see her again?"

"Probably."

We stepped into the hall. Laughter, music, and the scent of burgers floated from the common area.

He took my hand. "Let's go party."

"You go on. I'll be there in a minute."

"Everything okay?"

"Fine. I just need a minute. I want to change clothes and clean up a little."

"All right." He let go of my hand. "See ya in a few."

As he headed to the celebration, I made my way down the hall to my room. I dragged my suitcase from under my bed and opened it. As I pulled out a pair of jeans and a T-shirt, my gaze lingered on all my other clothes. I glanced over to my dresser and then back to my suitcase.

With a smile, I grabbed a wad of clothes, opened a dresser drawer, and tossed them inside. I snatched up another handful and threw them in, too. Then another, and another, and another.

Finishing up, I shoved the suitcase under my bed with a salute. "So long, suitcase. I'm home now. I'm here to stay."

GET A PEEK AT BOOK 2!

Using his homemade, handheld computer, the HOMAS B28, Frankie flipped through prescanned floor plans.

Impenetrable. That's what all the suppliers, media, and tech journals were bragging about the Rayver Security System.

We'll just see about that.

He tucked the B28 in his zippered thigh pocket and pulled out a granola bar.

Unwrapping it, Frankie studied the dark New Mexico Museum of History from the sidewalk. Easy enough to get in the front door. Standard nixpho lock with a keypad. Any kindergartener with half an IQ could do it, too.

He folded the chewy bar in half and shoved the whole thing in his mouth. Apple cinnamon. Not his favorite, but it was all the corner store had.

The true challenge of this job lay in the triple-sealed, flex-steel vault. Protected by the oh-so-impressive Rayver Security System.

Frankie didn't know what was in the vault. Didn't care.

He was here to crack the impenetrable Rayver System. No more, no less. Just to prove he could do it.

Tossing the wrapper in the already full garbage can, he crossed the shadowed street.

The two-story brick museum stood at the end of a long dead-end road with woods along the back and sides.

It was deserted. Too good to be true.

Frankie pulled his hood down over his face as he neared the entrance.

Five-five-six-four-three-zero. He punched in the code he'd seen the museum manager use every night this week. Anybody with binoculars and enough patience could've retrieved it, too.

Click. The door unlocked, and he slipped inside.

Standing in the entranceway, he scanned the dimly lit interior, recalling the layout. Left. Two rooms. Stairwell down. One room to the right.

"Okay, Frankie," he whispered to himself. "Game's on. Don't get too confident. Never know what might happen."

He closed his eyes and blew out a long slow breath. Then, with quiet feet, he shuffled left into the African Bone Room. A glass display case ran the center's length.

With his back to the west wall, he watched the corner camera. From his last visit to the museum, he recalled that it scanned in two-second intervals, moving a fraction of an inch to the right with each scan. He needed to make it across the room before it scanned back. No prob.

Staying in its blind spot, Frankie baby-stepped on each two-second interval and made it safely to the other side.

He entered the New Zealand Hat Room. No display cases here. No cameras either. Strange-looking hats hung on the walls, each rigged with an alarm should one be removed.

He squashed the mischievous urge to take one down

just to prove it could be done and crossed the carpet to the stairwell on the other side.

Suddenly, he stopped in midstep. Cold prickles crawled across his skin. *Somebody's in here.*

Slowly, he pivoted, searching every corner, shadow, and inch of space.

Nothing.

A good solid minute ticked by as he listened closely. Soft air-conditioner hum. Nearly inaudible camera ticks. Quiet laser alarm buzz.

Nothing else. No shuffle of a person's feet. No breath.

Funky imagination. That's all. Although he really didn't believe himself.

From his vest pocket Frankie pulled out a wad of home-made gray putty and a six-inch length of bamboo he used as a blowgun. Balling the putty, he fit it in the end of the bamboo.

The stairwell's camera hung catty-corner near the bottom. He rolled his black hood above his lips. Sighted down the length of the bamboo. Took a breath. Put it in his mouth. And blew.

The putty flew like a dart and plunked right on the lens.

Yeah, that's what I'm talking about.

He tiptoed down the stairs and hung a right, and his pulse jumped like it did every time a new security system challenged him.

The impenetrable Rayver System.

Impenetrable, his big toe.

He pulled his fiber-lit goggles used for laser detection from on top of his head and fit them over his eyes.

Bingo.

Yellow lasers zigzagged the room preceding the vault.

One-twothreefourfivesix . . . twenty ankle high. The same at waist. Six on the ceiling.

Child's play. Except for the yellow, skin-sizzling color. Whatever happened to the reliable red set-off-the-alarm-but-don't-fry-the-burglar color?

Leaning to the left at a seventy-degree angle, he spied a tunnel-like opening void of lasers. *You'd think the tech geniuses would've figured this out by now.*

Frankie unbuttoned a pocket in his cargo pants and pulled out the remote-control expander. Pointing it toward the opening of the tunnel, he pressed the expander button.

A skinny metal wire snaked out, becoming stiff as it left the remote control.

Steady, Frankie, steady.

One slight movement and the wire would collapse into the lasers.

It made it through the small tunnel void of lasers, across the room, and straight into the tiny hole below the vault's lock.

The lasers flicked off, and he set his watch. One minute and seventeen seconds until they turned back on.

Reeling in the expandable wire, he ran over the open tile to the vault. He yanked the tool kit from his vest and laid the triple-folded leather pouch on the ground. He took nitrox, a metal adhesive release, and squirted the control panel.

It popped off, and Frankie caught it before it clanged to the ground. Anything over twenty-five decibels would set off the alarm.

Multicolored wires crisscrossed and tangled with one another.

A diversion.

He reached in, grabbed the clump, and ripped them

right out. Red lasers immediately flicked on, filling the control panel opening.

Frankie took the extra-long needle-nose wire cutters from his tool pouch and, leaning to the left at a seventy-degree angle, found his opening.

Carefully, he inserted the wire cutters through the opening surrounded by lasers and snipped the one remaining white wire at the very back.

The vault clicked open. The control panel lasers flicked off. Frankie checked his watch.

Twenty seconds.

Snatching up the tools, he flung the vault door open. A small wooden man, an artifact of some sort, sat on a stand.

A weight-sensitive stand.

Crud.

He hadn't expected that.

Frankie estimated the artifact at three pounds and took three one-pound pellets from his tool pouch. Holding his breath, he slipped the artifact off and the pellets on all in one smooth motion.

And froze.

Nothing. Only silence.

No alarms. No lasers.

He checked his watch.

Three seconds.

Frankie sprinted back across the room. His watch alarm dinged. He dove the last few feet and whipped around to see the yellow lasers flick back on.

Whew.

Smiling, he did his victory shoulder-roll dance.

Oh, yeah. Frankie got it going on.

Go, Frankie. Go, Frankie. Go. Go.

He packed his stuff, slipped a yellow ribbon from his

sock, and tied it around the artifact. It was his signature. He wished he could be here to see them discover it outside its *impenetrable* vault.

With a pat to its head, he stood.

"Cute," a voice spoke.

Frankie spun around. Another person stood behind him.

Pointing a gun.

His heart stopped. Then he saw the gun shake.

Why . . . he's nervous.

The other guy flicked it toward the artifact. "Give it to me." Something distorted his voice.

Frankie ran his gaze down the length of the other burglar and back up. He looked like a skinnier version of Frankie. Black cargo pants and vest. Black hood. Black martial arts slippers.

"I said, give it to me."

Frankie shrugged. "Sure." Why did he care? He hadn't come for this silly thing anyway.

Behind the hood, the burglar narrowed his eyes, like he didn't believe it'd be that easy.

"It's all yours." Frankie stepped to the side.

The burglar paused. Shook his head. "Hand it to me."

Frankie sighed. "Oh, all right." He snatched it from the ground and tossed it to the burglar.

The burglar's eyes widened as he fumbled with the gun and caught the artifact.

Frankie watched him juggle the two things. He could totally take down this idiot. The burglar was *way* too amusing, though, and Frankie needed a good laugh.

Holding the artifact to his chest, the burglar scrambled to get the gun pointed back at Frankie. "You think you're funny don't you?"

He shrugged. Yeah, actually, he did.

The burglar backed his way up the stairs, still pointing the gun at Frankie.

"Can't fire that thing, ya know. You'll set off the alarms in this place."

The burglar paused in his backward ascent as if he hadn't thought about that. "You're the Ghost, aren't you?"

Frankie gave his best sixteenth-century bow. "The one and only."

"I . . . I've studied you."

The small admission pumped his ego. "Then you know I'm no threat. I did what I came for."

Seconds ticked by. The burglar slipped the gun inside his vest.

"Safety," Frankie reminded him.

"It's not loaded."

He laughed at having been tricked.

The burglar raced up the stairs toward the New Zealand Hat Room, and Frankie followed. With his back to the west wall, the burglar inched around the African Bone Room.

Frankie watched his fluid, timed movements as he kept pace with the camera that scanned in two-second intervals. Not such a novice. He'd been trained.

"Who are you?" Frankie whispered across both rooms.

The other burglar stopped and looked back.

"Keep moving!" Frankie hissed at the exact second the burglar missed his two-second step and set off the alarm.

Crud.

The burglar bolted from the room and up the steps to the second floor.

Frankie raced after him, through a narrow hallway into

a huge room, and then disappeared behind the door to a janitor closet.

Staying right on his heels, Frankie flung open the closet door. The burglar snaked up a rope hanging fifteen feet from an open skylight.

Quick guy.

He'd rigged the skylight alarm with an eraser, a small piece of aluminum foil, and, although Frankie couldn't see it, he knew a dab of olive oil. That particular combination of three elements shorted out standard valumegal wiring. He'd introduced that five years ago, and criminals had copied it ever since.

Sirens filtered through the air, and his pulse jumped. Cops. About a quarter of a mile away.

Yeah, baby, thrill of the chase.

The burglar made it to the roof, and Frankie started his ascent. Halfway there he looked up to see the burglar holding a knife to the rope.

No.

"Sorry," the burglar mumbled, and sliced it clean.

Son of a— Frankie fell and landed on his back. "Umph."

Footsteps pounded outside the door. He jumped to his feet and leapt for the skylight.

The door flew open. "Hold it right there."

Frankie froze and squeezed his eyes shut.

Crud. Double crud.

"Put your hands up."

He stuck his hands in the air. *I'm going to prison for this.*

"Now turn around. *Real* slow."

Opening his eyes, Frankie pivoted.

Someone yanked off his hood and shined a light in his face. Frankie squinted.

"Well, look here. You're just a kid." The cop jerked

Frankie's arms back and handcuffed him. "You have the right to remain silent. . . ." The cop hauled Frankie through the museum and out the door.

As the cop shoved Frankie in the squad car, Frankie glanced toward the woods. The burglar stood in the shadows, watching.

FROM THE AUTHOR

Things you should know about me: I write novels! Some have won awards. Others have been bestsellers. Under Shannon Greenland (my real name) you'll find spies, adventure, and romance. Under S. E. Green (my pen) you'll find dark and gritty fiction about serial killers, cults, secret societies that do bad things, and whatever else my twisted brain deems to dream up.

I'm on Instagram, Twitter, and Facebook. I also have a website and a very non-annoying newsletter where you can keep up to date with new releases, take advantage of free stuff, and read along with my mild ramblings about my travels. I love old dogs. My humor runs dark and so don't be offended by something off I might say. I mean no harm. I live in a small Florida beach town but I'm most often found exploring the world. I eat entirely too many chips. I also love math!

BOOKS BY SHANNON GREENLAND

THE SPECIALISTS SERIES

Model Spy

Down to the Wire

The Winning Element

Native Tongue

Fight to the Finish

THE SUMMER MY LIFE BEGAN

Em

Gwenny

PIPER INVESTIGATIONS

The Case of The Bad Twin

The Gator in a Tux

The Island Mafia